AF570382

AMERICAN EARTHQUAKES

AMERICAN EARTHQUAKES

A NOVEL BY CONSTANCE URDANG

COFFEE HOUSE PRESS :: MINNEAPOLIS :: 1988

This project is supported in part by Elmer and Eleanor Andersen; The Dayton Hudson Foundation with funds from Dayton's and Target Stores; The National Endowment for the Arts; a federal agency; Star Tribune/Cowles Media Company; and United Arts. The publisher thanks Minnesota Center for Book Arts, where Coffee House has been a Visiting Press since 1985.

Coffee House Press books are available through our exclusive trade distributor: CONSORTIUM BOOK SALES AND DISTRIBUTION, 213 East Fourth Street, St. Paul, Minnesota 55101. Our books are also available through all major library distributors and jobbers, and through most small press distributors, including Bookpeople, Inland, Pacific Pipeline, and Small Press Distribution. For personal orders, catalogs, or other information, write to: COFFEE HOUSE PRESS, Post Office Box 10870, Minneapolis, Minnesota 55458.

Library of Congress Cataloging in Publication Data

Urdang, Constance.
American Earthquakes : a novel / by Constance Urdang
p. cm.
ISBN 0-918273-42-0 (pbk. : alk. paper) : $9.95
I. Title.
PS3571.R3A84 1988
813'.54–dc 19 88-11890

CIP

I

Wisdom and Practice

Edmund, a surgeon on the hospital staff, is thinking about the wisdom of the Church, which canonized St. Martin of Tours: " . . . met a beggar almost naked and frozen with cold . . . cut his cloak in two and gave him half. That night he saw Our Lord clothed in the half cloak and heard him say to the angels, 'Martin, yet a catechumen, hath wrapped me in this garment.'"

When Martin Conrad, his best friend and confidant of his soul in high school, brought to his attention the story of his namesake, Edmund had been shaken and revolted. Afraid even then of seeming to be naive, he had said nothing to his friend, but secretly he thought the Church cynical to the point of hypocrisy to confer sainthood on a man, even in the fifteenth century, who had been so lacking in generosity as to give only half his cloak to the beggar. Half a cloak, it seemed to him, he himself would have been able to give. If it had been the whole cloak—then, a saint, a saint without a doubt.

Now, twenty-five years later and still an apostate, it seems to him that in this story as in no other, the Church demonstrates her infinite compassion. Sometimes he thinks it was this very story that made him decide to choose plastic surgery as his specialty. It still hurts him when people smile knowingly on learning what he does, as though the only conceivable reason for such a choice were the lure of gain, money. "No, no, not really that at all—or hardly at all," he qualifies his statement.

Even the more sympathetic of his acquaintances make the mistake of assuming, once they are over the money hurdle, that he is chiefly concerned with victims of massive disfigurement, children grotesquely malformed at birth, or young girls hideously scarred or burned, victims of some Hiroshima in their own country or elsewhere; it isn't so. Not that he is unstirred by these innocent martyrs, but after all, they will come to their reward with or without his ministrations. His primary concern is with the less dramatically wounded, the little sparrows, sullen girls with overlarge noses or receding chins, spoiled, unhappy women who yearn to be young again, the vast uncounted army of the discontented, who yet believe it is in his power to heal and save them. He himself knows how illusory their hopes of him are, and yet . . . and yet . . .

"It's not altogether useless," he tells himself, "to restore whatever beauty you can to the ugly world . . . no more pointless, after all, than putting on theatricals . . . or making statues or pictures . . ."

Causerie

"Doctors always hate pathologists, that's why Hobart is always having to find new ones," he says playfully. He is having coffee in the hospital cafeteria with Binnie and Vera.

"Why are you saying this?" asks Vera seriously. Fluent as it is, her English can never keep up with Edmund's nuances.

"Because the pathologist shows up their mistakes. He's the one with the last word; he does the autopsies."

"You are not being serious, it is only your humor of the macabre," Vera reproaches him.

"Not at all. For one thing, my macabre humor is always most serious. And for another, doctors are human, my dear Vera, they don't like it when their mistakes are recalled from beyond the grave. Even Hobart is human."

"Now I know you are joking." Vera's manner is severe; she doesn't like it when doctors are made fun of, or when their reliability is questioned.

Binnie interposes, "But *you* don't have any reason to hate them, Edmund—your mistakes aren't fatal."

"Not as a rule," Edmund says drily.

Vera's Prescription

A short, dumpy figure wearing some sort of jacket-and-skirt and sensible shoes, somewhat untidy about the hair, which remains a rich, unlikely shade of auburn, and with eyes unexpectedly keen and frostily blue, Vera is an occupational therapist at the hospital, a job for which she trained when she first came to the United States in 1940 as a refugee from Hitler's Austria. Now, almost thirty years later, unofficially she holds the position of lay confessor to patients and staff alike.

Vera told Hobart, "The best thing would be, for Louise, to start doing her sculpture again, and I think, if she were not an artist by profession, she would do it. There is nothing, physically, to prevent her. But for a sculptor, sculpture isn't occupational therapy, something to fill up the time, to give a sense of achievement. For her . . . it is that, but it is something else also, something that has to come from inside. You can't force her. If I insist, if I say to her, 'You have to do this in order to help your leg to heal,' she will go through the motions, yes. And she will probably produce something that looks better than what a less talented person would produce, but she will suffer from it. It will not help her in her mind. All we can do with her now is wait. When she is ready, she will begin again."

Earthquakes in Missouri

fall on a line of epicenters extending to the St. Lawrence Seaway
New Mad-rid (as the locals call it) to all intents and purposes unpopulated at the time of the biggest earthquake ever reported on the North American continent, lies on the Missouri side of a bend in the Mississippi about 200 miles south of St. Louis. If a seismic disturbance comparable in magnitude to that of 1811 were to occur there today, extensive property damage and loss of life would result.

Louise traces with her finger the faint dotted lines on the newspaper map that mark the three major geologic faults underlying the region.

. . . strong northeast fault trend . . . extends to the eastern border . . . aligning with the trend . . . on the earthquake epicenter map . . .
north of New Madrid . . . a major fault . . . parallels the Pascola Arch . . . these trends intersect . . .

Louise's Success

Louise is Hobart's wife, a lanky, loose-limbed blonde, given to large gestures and generous enthusiasms. She is a sculptor, quirky and idiosyncratic, very successful in the New York world of galleries and critics (which she rarely visits), a world of which her neighbors, Hobart's medical colleagues, and, in fact, Hobart himself, are largely unaware. She works, or did before the accident, in what she calls Steel Direct, wearing a mask and asbestos gloves, using a torch to bend and twist steel rods into the very shapes of her imagination.

From Twisted

pipe, steel rods, ashes and charred fragments, Louise J____ constructs tragic icons that are. . . vestiges of doomed souls, devitalized man. . . . her art in relation to the idea of the theatre of the absurd. . . tragedy and comedy merge and interact . . .

strong sense of historical style, despite the anti-finish of her surfaces. . . desiccated personages . . . inseparable from their emotional context . . . forces our sensibilities . . .

this rawness of imagery

Hanging Figure
Hanging Man
Torn Figure
Screaming Figure
Study for Screaming
Sundered Images
Broken Man
Two Figures with Broken Figure

The Three Aunts

Binnie's three old aunts were still living together in the same apartment where the oldest, Helen, had lived first with both her parents and then with her invalid mother. The youngest, Tess, was the first to return, having lost her husband (by death) and her daughter Grace (by marriage).

"And I'll tell you, Binnie, I'm certainly glad she did," Grace told her cousin during one of their infrequent tête-à-têtes. "Otherwise I'd have lived in mortal fear that she'd want to move in with us. Because anyone can see my mother is simply incapable of living by herself. And—leaving Susie out of it altogether—I know I absolutely could not handle it."

Susie was Grace's daughter and only child, produced nine months after Grace's marriage, six months after Walter's induction into the army, and five years before the divorce.

"It's certainly fortunate we didn't have any more kids," says Grace. "Between worrying about her killing herself by accident and her getting busted, I hardly have a free moment as it is, with one. Thank goodness she's a girl – I didn't have to cope with the draft."

Ethel, the middle sister, moved in with the other two when she was widowed after forty years of marriage. Like her husband, Ralph, she had been a doctor; she was already half-retired at the time of Ralph's death. Afterward she gradually gave up what was left of her practice and finally stopped going to the hospital altogether. Nevertheless, her move surprised everyone. The three sisters had never got on really well together, although they had achieved a kind of balance during the years when each had lived her separate life, meeting only at Thanksgiving, Christmas, and family birthdays.

Standing in that cramped, scrubbed lobby, tiled with its green and yellow lotus and papyrus motifs, smelling formidably of disinfectant, Binnie always felt a chill. Somebody walking over her grave, her aunt Tessie's old laundress (long since in her own) would have said. She wondered how could all three have come back to live in the place from which, as girls, they must surely have dreamed of escaping. She had never been able to understand why Helen came back from New York, or how she could have stayed on in the apartment, first with her widowed mother (ten years an invalid), and then, particularly then – after Mom-mom's death, alone, solitary in the house where she would always be a daughter.

"As if nothing had ever happened."

The Richter scale measures ground motion as recorded on seismographs. An earthquake recorded as five is capable of causing considerable damage. A seven reading indicates a major quake, one that can cause widespread, heavy damage, and an eight is a great earthquake. The San Francisco quake of 1906, which occurred before the formulation of the Richter scale, is estimated to have probably measured around eight.

Helen Is Stricken

Waking in what she recognizes instantly as a room in the hospital, Helen's first thought is, "Well, it's happened, at last."

She lies motionless for an interval, watching the faintly fiery glow of sunlight making a pattern on the wall through the slotted blind.

"I don't even know if it's morning or afternoon – which way does this window face? Am I watching a sunrise or a sunset?"

She contemplates ringing for the nurse to ask the time, but the effort of raising and turning her head, lifting her arm to feel for the bell she knows must be near the head of the bed, defeats her. "I don't even know what day it is."

Heart attack? Stroke? Accident? What caused her to be brought here? She has no memory, only the awakening.

"After all, it's all the same," she thinks. Another half hour and the question will answer itself. Either the room will brighten, and the fiery patterns pale and be diffused to daylight, or the window will finally go black. She dozes.

Helen's Escape

Oddly enough, it had been neither of the two world wars that freed Helen from what she had thought of at the time as her father's benevolent despotism (although much later, after his death, she came to see that it was her mother's thinly veiled tyranny that had held them both, Papa as well as herself). When the boys she had known in high school enlisted and went away during the First World War to fight in the trenches of Flanders something came over her, and without telling anyone, she applied for training and for overseas duty as an administrative hospital aide. No one could have been more surprised than she when she received a notice requiring her to report to Chicago for training.

Chicago!

Her mother wept and had a gall bladder attack, and Papa shouted and threatened and, finally, reminded her that she was not of age. She had lied about her age on the application. So nothing came of it after all.

The Baby of the Family

Tessie was always the baby, dressed up, petted, given special treats. It never occurred to anyone that she would not finish high school, although it had been a struggle for Helen and Ethel—in those days school wasn't taken for granted for girls—and then, no sooner did she graduate (and wasn't she the prettiest girl in the class, all curls and dimples, in her ruffled white dress?) than she announced that she and Leon were going to be married right away.

"It's just as well; no office would put up with her and her ways;" Ethel muttered disloyally, adding, "at least now she'll be supported in the style to which she'd like to be accustomed. But you'd think she could have waited just a little bit." Ethel, who wanted desperately to go on studying so she could go to medical school some day, was working in an office and hating it. Helen, the oldest, was the only one who had done what Papa wanted: stayed home to help Mom-mom.

Forty-four years later, Helen wondered, "Would it really have made much difference if Papa had let me go to work the way I wanted to? As things turned out it didn't matter – it was the war that changed everything, after all."

Everything except Tessie. After two world wars, a depression, motherhood, widowhood, grandmotherhood, she is still the baby: corseted, with eyes painted like Cleopatra, wearing a blue-tinted wig, teetering along on the spike heels that no one, not Leon, not Grace, not Helen and Ethel, has been able to get her to forego, she dimples and pouts, squeals, gasps, gurgles, snatches and holds, is as greedy, sly, ruthless, charming, and stubborn as ever.

"How is it possible to live so long and learn so little?" Ethel once said, marvelling at her sister, to her husband, Ralph.

"What she learned early is that it works," Ralph had replied.

A Shower of Gold

It's not only in St. Louis that sometimes on a raw, blustery day in October or November a particular tree may suddenly lose all its leaves at once, letting go of them all together in a shower of gold, but for Binnie, who had seen it happen as she waited one day for Rich in the hospital courtyard, it became peculiarly associated with their relationship. She never forgot it.

Binnie has never been the kind of girl who giggles and confides, who pours out into the ear of a best friend who kissed and how much and where, or how far above or below the waist she allowed his hand to stray. Like many only children, she has a strong sense of privacy. During her childhood, perpetually on guard against adult invasion, her bedroom door bristled with signs: "Keep Out," "No Trespassing," "This Means You." Her drawers were full of notebooks labelled "Private," "Do Not Open," "Secret and Confidential," "Top (Most) Secret."

So she has never confided in her closest friend, Sarah, in spite of all the years they shared each other's morning coffee sessions in the hospital cafeteria; in spite of the nylons and blouses and strapless bras borrowed and lent, the steamy girl-to-girl sessions in her apartment or Sarah's (across the hall) while putting up their hair on rollers, turning up hems, cooking dinners in each other's kitchenettes; in spite of Sarah's copious reports on her progress with Bob during the first months of their acquaintance, then on their honeymoon and (while she continued to work at the hospital) on her in-laws, her attempts to get pregnant, and finally – in the last months before she stopped working and moved out into the suburb where Robin was born – the daily log of the stormy seas of her pregnancy. When they meet now, of course, things aren't quite the same, although Sarah continues to admonish and advise and unburden herself over coffee or sherry while the baby naps.

"Are you still seeing Rich?"

"Yes . . ."

The New Doctor

"Have you met the new member of our staff, the pathologist?" somebody at the hospital asked Binnie.

"Not yet, but I did hear they'd found one."

"His name is Derek Trudman. He's supposed to be very sharp. Black, you know."

"He'd have to be sharp. I'm surprised Semple agreed—or didn't he have anything to say about it?" Hobart would make the final decision, of course.

Edmund said slyly, "And even if Hobart is as much of a racist as Semple, he can't admit it. Not even to himself. Hiring a black staff member is his way of camouflaging his real feelings."

"Edmund, you're impossible," said Binnie. "As far as you're concerned, he's damned if he does and damned if he doesn't. I thought you were such good friends with Hobart and Louise."

"I am, I am," said Edmund, "and I can't wait to meet Dr. Trudman. So far, I've only admired him from afar."

A Drink Before Dinner

Hobart hopefully repeats to Louise, in his measured, cadenced manner (which really is quite effective and soothing with his patients), what Vera has said—to which she replies, explosively, "Bullshit!" and throws the book she has been reading, which happens to be Francoise Gilot's *Life with Picasso*, on the floor.

She is repentant.

"I really didn't mean to do that, darling, it simply flew out of my hand."

She allows him to pick it up and put it on the already

crowded table next to her chair.

"I like Vera, she's a good, kind woman, but how can I do anything now that I'm a cripple? Can't you just see me hopping around with my blowtorch? I wish all those 'helpful-hannahs' and 'meddling-marys' over at your hospital would leave me alone. They've done enough damage."

Hobart knows better than to say anything to this. He starts to mix himself a drink.

"How about one for you?" he asks over his shoulder, swirling the ice cubes around in his glass with his finger.

"That's something I can still do," she says ungraciously. "At least you can still drink sitting down."

What Has Happened

Nobody in St. Louis knows what Helen did or even where she lived when she left home and went to New York in the twenties. She didn't return for almost a quarter of a century, until after World War II. Then she came back for her father's funeral and stayed on to take care of her invalid mother, who was expected to follow him into the grave within the month, but instead lingered for ten years.

"My mother always thought she must have met some man there and they got married secretly," Tess's daughter Grace has told her cousin Binnie.

"But why would she have to keep it secret? I should think your grandfather and Mom-mom would have been pleased if she got married–wasn't that what girls were supposed to do? And even if they disapproved–she was of age," Binnie argued.

"I agree, but that's what Mother thought. She still does," said Grace.

"Maybe she was living in sin," Binnie suggested.

They giggled like adolescents.

A Freak Case

All the doctors agree that Louise is a freak case. Something like this doesn't happen once in two hundred years – and especially not in these days of penicillin, aureomycin, antibiotics, antisepsis, the advances of modern medicine. Kidney machines, heart transplants. If anything, Hobart finds, this sort of talk makes Louise even more bitter.

"Why me?"

She is not at all interested in the investigation of the series of events – unforeseeable events – that led to the amputation of her leg.

"All I know is, I'm a cripple."

"First of all," Hobart explains to her, "it's not so uncommon for someone who hauls heavy pieces of metal and pipe around to drop one on a foot sooner or later. You know that as well as I do. Plenty of narrow escapes you've had! So this once, it shattered the bone."

"I know all about it," grates Louise.

"But they know all about that kind of thing now, and after all, ours is one of the finest hospitals in the country. You were lucky."

She says nothing.

"Nobody could have predicted that you would get a staph infection, and that it would be a resistant strain. You know they tried everything – everything. They did it to save your life; there wasn't any choice. Louise – "

"Get the hell out of here," replies his loving wife.

Fabricated From

. . . torn paper, tangled wire, sheets of cast rubber, dyed canvas, metal, squares and wedges of polyester resin,

and twisted pipe . . .
Events
occurrences
incidents
Concerns
contingencies
crises
Facts and phenomena
Anything that impels, impends, impinges
accidents
adventures
Consequences
had taken it right in the face.
His eyes have already been operated on twice and the doctor
. . . nothing left
in the other one, it just exploded
The doctor said there
are pellets lodged in the brain
Had to wait 90 minutes
The police are doing a good job, he said

Rates of Violence

The following scale of the classification of the different rates of violence has been constructed.

1. First Rate. Most tremendous, so as to threaten the destruction of the town, and which would soon effect it, should the action continue with the same degree of violence. Buildings oscillate largely and irregularly and grind against each other, the walls split and begin to yield, chimneys, parapets, and gable-ends break in various directions and topple to the ground.
2. Second Rate. Less violent, but severe.
3. Third Rate. Moderate, but sufficient to be alarming to

people generally.

4. Fourth Rate. Perceptible to the feelings of those who are still and not subject to other motion or sort of jarring that might resemble this.
5. Fifth Rate. Although often causing a strange sort of sensation, and sometimes giddiness, the motion is not to be ascertained positively; but by vibrators or other objects, either placed for that purpose, or disposed accidentally, it can be detected.

The Spiders

In one of her rare bursts of confidence, Grace's daughter Sue told Binnie, "Sometimes . . . ever since I was a little kid . . . it gives me the shudders . . . I think my mother . . . and my grandmother . . . and yes, even Mom-mom, she was my great-grandmother . . . were all spiders.

"Maybe it started because they used to call me Miss Muffet, and tease me. . . 'along came a spider and sat down beside her' . . . ugh . . .

"Spiders, devouring the male after they mated.

"We're a family of spiders . . . you too, Binnie . . . don't let it happen . . . I don't want to be one."

Was Ethel Ever a Girl?

Was Ethel ever a girl? Yes, Ethel was a girl for a very long time before she took up the study of medicine, before she met Ralph and brought forth sons. For many years she forced sugarwater down the tiny throats of moribund nestlings, splinted starlings' wings, smeared mange-ridden dogs or torn and bleeding tomcats with ointment or unguent, tied bandages, tweezed out thorns and porcupine quills. She also fed strays and wept and held funerals over those who succumbed. In the loamy back yard she made a cemetery with painted tombstones in the soft earth of a disused flowerbed, and she took care of her baby sister Tessie whenever Mom-mom asked her to, although she was not the oldest. She liked to play Mother. Even when they were quite small and played house, Ethel was always the mother. Her older sister Helen was Baby, and often Tessie was the cat. Sometimes Helen would agree to be Father, but when she did he always went away to sea, or even further, to explore the Nile or the Amazon, and the mother and baby left behind at home had nothing to do, or had to be sailors or explorers all afternoon.

The Generation Gap

Binnie, who is thirteen years older than Sue, thinks Sue's decision not to go back to school next semester is wrong.

"I'm old enough to see—they throw themselves away, they spend themselves, yes, that's exactly the right word, they spend as if there'll always be more where that came from, as if the reckoning will never come." Binnie is frightened, not for Sue, but for herself.

Sue says, "They need clerical help so badly, I bet even with my lousy typing, if I went to someone and asked, they'd hire me."

She says, "All the kids who got factory jobs got promoted very fast, as soon as the supervisors found out they were intelligent. The kids said you wouldn't believe how dumb most people are."

Binnie says, "I don't expect a really classy job with a carpet on the floor or anything to start, just an ordinary minimum wage job . . . even waitressing." She adds, "Kids make more than a hundred bucks a week in tips alone at some of these places. Sure the boss is a bastard, but so what?"

Time is what. What will defeat them. Binnie knows how deceptive time is, how seemingly innocent, how relentless.

Binnie weeps for the defeat of the kids by time. For Sue. For herself. Is she already defeated, she wonders.

Ethel's Dilemma

Ethel says earnestly to Vera, "I know I'm not brilliant—never have been. But sometimes I think I've got something to offer—for that very reason, maybe."

She always feels inexperienced in Vera's presence, as if Vera's having lived through World War II in a concentration camp has marked her in a very special way, has given her a depth of compassion that Ethel herself could never attain, although she believes she admires it. What she has never been able to admit to herself is that she has this feeling with regard to all Jews. They need not be European, or even to have suffered, as she knows, vaguely, Vera has suffered. She felt this even about Ralph, her husband, although in that relation her response to his Jewishness was inextricably entangled with the unexpressed—inexpressible—complexity and confusion of all her responses to their life together. How could she ever suffer enough?

"I used to think that by the time I got to this point in my life—by the time people got to this point in their lives—one would see things more clearly. But it isn't that way at all," she says to Vera.

"Also, the world too has become more complicated," Vera agrees, puffing on her inevitable lipstick-stained cigarette and flapping her other hand rapidly in front of her face to dissipate the smoke in her characteristic gesture.

"I do want to do something, though, now that I've retired. Ralph wouldn't have wanted me to–I'm not ready to settle down in a rocking chair. My training–" after all, she is a doctor.

"Of course you are right," Vera says warmly. "Are you thinking of something special to do?"

"I was hoping you might have a suggestion."

May Not Be the Same

as actual movement
. . . violently shaken in the near future, but he asked, "What
is the near future?
PROPHECIES AFTER THE EVENT
used in conversation by people who don't know
what a Happening is
RELATED TO MAPPED FAULTS
bleeding and with broken limbs
against a pitiful background of groans and
cries and the frantic agonies of wounded animals
DID NOTHING TO HELP
"It ruins the whole mood when you have to get up and cook
a meal or something in the middle of it," she said *POW*
(playing the piano with the bloody *SMASH*
carcass of a chicken) *ZAP*
BOOM *BANG*
ANGER AND DISGUST
obstinate
people who would not *seek safety and* had to *be*
abandoned
thought the great building would collapse
on their heads

AFTERSHOCKS OF RICHTER MAGNITUDE 3.3
(never even bothered to clean the tables afterwards and then later on would even eat at those same
CLASSIFICATION OF FAULTS

Nobody has ever actually found the New Madrid fault, which is believed to lie buried deep in the alluvial soil of the Mississippi River valley. Its precise location is not indicated on any geological survey maps, for unlike the San Andreas fault, whose course may be clearly traced on an aerial photograph of the region, the New Madrid fault betrays no hint of its presence on the earth's surface.

The Mirror

Helen, twenty-four years old, stared at herself in the big, old-fashioned mirror in the big, old-fashioned bedroom she had all to herself now that both her sisters were married, Ethel just last week, and cried, "But what if nothing ever happens?"

The Valedictory

Two weeks later, having packed her valise in secret, and withdrawn the money from her savings account (the passbook had been in her possession since her twenty-first birthday) Helen was on her way to New York. The money, all except what she needed for her one-way ticket and the expenses of the trip, was securely tucked into a special cloth belt she wore fastened around her waist under her skirt—it had a firm, reassuring feel.

She had told no one, not even her sisters (who, in any case, were busy, Tessie getting ready for the birth of her baby, and Ethel off on her honeymoon with Ralph) of her plans, until the very morning of her departure, coming into the diningroom for breakfast, already drawing on her gloves, the train scheduled to leave within the hour.

Chewing earnestly, Papa had raised one eyebrow, snorted, and said, briefly, "Idiotic!"

Mom-mom, after an initial gasp, kept repeating, "No, Helen, no, this is a terrible thing, you must not be so headstrong, a step like this can't be taken in a hurry."

She pressed one hand to her bosom and reached out to her husband, now drinking his morning coffee, with the other.

"Tell her, Papa, tell her!"

"Tell her! There's nothing to tell. She wants to leave – let her go." He waved the importunate hand away, set his oversize cup back in its saucer, and blotted his lips with a clean napkin.

"She wants to go – goodby."

Mom-mom, having found a handkerchief, wept.

And Helen, torn, distracted, faintly nauseated with emotion, gave up trying to begin to explain.

"There's the taxi – I'll miss my train!"

She ran first to her father, then her mother, embraced them both, and flung herself through the door, across the veranda, down the steps, along the walk, and, finally, into the cab.

Louise's Accident

It sometimes seems to Louise that the very grotesqueness – the absurdity – of her accident has something to do with the times we live in. As though a nobler age would not have produced suffering so bizarre and even laughable.

Sometimes she even finds herself rehearsing, in her mind, the actual incident, as if by reliving those few minutes she could somehow change the outcome. It had not—and that was somehow one of the things about it that she most resented—seemed especially important at the time. Even the pain was not unbearable. And it was so quickly over. Only a few seconds for the thing to slip and fall on her foot, a sensation of a tremendous weight pinning her foot to the ground. And then she managed, somehow, to free it, hopping from the studio to the house. Not five minutes had elapsed—she was sure of it—between the time when it actually fell and the moment she sank into the chair next to the telephone and dialed Hobart at the hospital.

Nor was there much blood. Only the unnatural angle at which her foot hung from the ankle, only the beginnings of sensation in the damaged leg, more like the anticipation of pain than pain itself.

And what happened next had no aura of tragedy about it either. It hardly seemed worth calling it an emergency. Just that Hobart, who appeared on the scene with the ambulance men, had directed them to the emergency room as a matter of course. Xrays, naturally. Warmth and medication, first for the shock, and then to forestall the pain that the doctors knew would follow.

What followed?

Chiefly, Louise thinks, boredom. Impatience, irritability, restlessness. The difficulty, above all the tedium, of remaining immobile.

They provided her with a wheelchair, but somehow it only seemed to emphasize her enforced passivity. Where could she go? Nowhere. The hospital remained nothing but an enormous limbo, in which it made no difference whether she was in one part or another. She could do nothing. Full of loathing for herself and the other patients, she would wheel herself down to the solarium, where all day long and much of the night the TV glared and gibbered, the ashtrays were full of cigarette butts and stank, and the magazines, much thumbed and little read, were got through in no time at all. How she detested the patronizing cheerfulness of the women and girls who wheeled library books, newspapers, toothpaste, cologne, and candy in and out of the dozens of rooms along the pale green corridor. How she despised her roommate, a massive old lady with a broken hip, who believed that every cloud has a silver lining.

Boredom.

She scarcely noticed when the doctors began looking worried as they examined the wound that didn't heal beneath the sterile dressings.

She had no feeling of urgency, no heightened consciousness, no premonition of disaster. Not once was she aware of herself as the central figure in a tragedy.

"Ridiculous!" she exclaimed when Hobart broke the news of the necessary amputation – and that was what it continued to seem to her – ridiculous. Not catastrophic, not disastrous, not tragic.

The Younger Generation

"Oh, *wow*," says Susie. "That's really Karmic."

For a minute Binnie thinks she has said "comic," and is startled; when she realizes what she has actually heard, she shakes her head rapidly from side to side as if to clear it, remembering this as a gesture of Ethel's from her own girlhood.

She looks at Sue, seeing her as a predestined victim of contemporary girlhood: rape and murder.

Doctor and Patient

"My dear girl, you wouldn't believe," Edmund says, "some of the things I hear, being privy to the secrets of the female heart."

He pauses to fish out a platinum cigarette case from an inner pocket of his immaculately pressed white coat.

Binnie says, "I daresay I wouldn't."

"One of my patients, I wouldn't dream of telling her name, God forbid, you might meet her some day, professional ethics and all that sort of thing – a very attractive woman, and married to quite a nice fellow, really, I don't know why they have to tell me these things."

He pauses again, lights the cigarette, and goes on, "I hardly know whether to believe her or not, masturbating with an electric toothbrush – really. Talk about Sodom and Gomorrah, they just weren't in it." He leans forward, confidentially. "Do you think she was trying to tell me something?"

The St. Louis earthquake of 1969, which measured 5.3 on the Richter scale, probably represented displacement at a depth of about 19 km. along the Centerville fault zone, and was related to mapped faults in an area of southern Illinois along the Kentucky border near Harrisburg, where the center was determined to be. It was felt over an area of more than 400,000 square miles.

To the layman, even the notion of earthquakes in Missouri is bizarre. No doubt, scientists, geologists, perhaps, whose business it is to explain what they do not understand, have discovered something to account for it. But what do these pleasantly rolling, undistinguished acres have in common with the wild, tumbled landscapes of Turkey or Peru? Even the Pacific littoral or the Italian Alps seem a more appropriate locale for subterranean violence. The experts agree that it is not always possible to determine, from a superficial look at the topography of a region, where the buried faults lie, although the trained eye can learn to recognize areas of past or future stress.

Helen's Good Intentions

Hard to believe that this hospital room faces the same way as her girlhood room in her parents' house, but the sun rising in the morning comes in at the window in the same way, making rosy patterns on the wall and ceiling. Helen can lie abed watching them as she has not been able to do since those girlhood days, when time itself was timeless and every day stretched before her like a desert—unmapped, untravelled, infinite in its possibilities.

These days too extend limitlessly before her, featureless and empty. The incessant busyness of the hospital routine, from student nurses with trays full of thermometers upright in alcohol-filled containers, to the squabbling cleaning-women in the corridor, the impersonally cheerful dietician, attendants with washbasins, bad-complexioned boys with trays of lukewarm food, interns, doctors—all these succeed in so breaking into her consciousness that she feels she is no longer capable of coherent thought.

Every morning she thinks, "Now that I'm allowed to sit up, I'll make an effort, take down some notes, get something in writing—" She has always meant to write a book about Wolf Tombey—but the day slips by, the effort is too great, the interruptions too many. She lies propped on pillows in a kind of dream, unable even to feel regret when, by the arrival of the evening meal, the final temperature-taking, and the entry of the dispensing nurse with her sleeping potions, she is forced to recognize that another day has passed and nothing has been accomplished. Night has fallen.

Unable to regret the wasted hours, she composes herself obediently to sleep, thinking only, "Tomorrow, then. Tomorrow I'll make the effort, make some notes, do some writing, get started."

Wolf's Life

For years Helen had kept in the back of her mind the possibility that someday she would write a book about Wolf's life, just as she kept in the back of her closet roped cartons of the letters and papers he had sent her, and in the basement storeroom the metal filing cases and heavy brown paper bags full of papers and notebooks she had taken from his room after he died. When she left New York she moved all these papers with her, and now they were crowded into the closets and cupboards of the apartment she shared with Ethel and Tessie. Sometimes, looking at the bundles of letters and manuscripts, she thought Wolf must never have thrown anything away. He had kept papers not out of caution or nostalgia, but because it was easier to let them accumulate than to sort them out.

Prodded by the lawyers, she had gone through some of them, but it was clear that his estate did not amount to enough to make straightening it out profitable to anyone, and then the war put purely literary matters out of her head. By the time the war was over, the fashion in poets had changed, Wolf had faded into obscurity, and publishers were no longer interested in the possibility of unearthing a posthumous volume. This, combined with her own disinclination to stir up the past while it still had the power to hurt her, led Helen to ignore the contents of her closets. But now suddenly the idea stirred again. Why not?

The Three Fates

"When we were girls," Helen once said to Binnie, "we liked to call ourselves the Three Fates."

"Not the Three Graces?" teased Binnie, keyed up as she was, awaiting Rich's call, conscious of marking time in her aunt's apartment. "Not the Muses?"

"There were nine muses," Helen said reprovingly, but her mouth had twitched. "Not at all. We liked to think of ourselves—oh, it was self-dramatizing—as daughters of night and sisters of the goddess of death—it appealed to us in those days."

"Which one were you?" Binnie lit another cigarette, glancing at her wristwatch as she did it.

"Atropos, I think, the one with the shears—she cuts off the thread. Tessie was Clotho, and Ethel was Lachesis. Clotho is the spinner, and Lachesis is the one who casts the lots—"

To Binnie, who had a hard time imagining her staid, elderly aunts in such romantic poses, it presented itself as a scene out of an old daguerreotype album. Suddenly she saw the three girls posturing in the middle distance on a lawn, next to a prop plaster pillar, in long-ago sunlight, almost as if she were looking at an actual picture.

But of course there is no such picture. Helen was thinking, "No, that isn't right, Ethel was Atropos—unturning, inflexible—the one that Plato said sings of the future. Because that was the way we always thought of her; she was the one who had her life all mapped out. And Tessie was Lachesis, who sings of the past, and I was the spinner—" her thoughts drifted on. "But now I'm the one who sings of the past, it's safe there. Everything was safer then."

Aloud she said, "We never used to have all these muggings, purse-snatchings, and things like that in this neighborhood. It gets worse all the time—did you know, Mrs. Dermott was knocked down last week right in front of this building and they took her purse?"

Binnie was shocked. Now she would have to start worrying about the aunts, she thought guiltily. "What happened?"

"Well, luckily, her son was home, and he heard her call out. He rushed outside and scared them off immediately—two young men, it was. But suppose he hadn't been there? It took the police twenty-five minutes to get here."

"Did they catch the men?" Binnie stubbed out her cigarette—she hadn't really wanted it anyway. As she did it, the phone rang. "Shall I—I'm expecting a call—" She didn't wait to hear Helen's reply; the telephone was in the foyer.

When she came back into the living room she was already pushing her arms into her coat, gathering up cigarettes and lighter, her gloves, her red scarf. "Aunt Helen, I've got to rush off, I'm sorry—"

Helen stood up, smoothing her skirt with crooked fingers, and Binnie put an arm around her thin shoulder, a quick hug, but she wasn't really sorry to be leaving; her blood sang, it buzzed in her ears, she wanted to fly.

"Goodby, Binnie dear, come again," her aunt Helen had said; she stood in the sunlight near the mute canary's cage. As Binnie hurried out she could hear the telephone ringing again, and the thought, "There, she *isn't* alone, it's foolish to feel as if I'm deserting her, they have their own lives," and she flew down the stairs to her meeting with Rich.

Her Own Life

On the long train ride across Ohio, Pennsylvania, New York, and, finally, down the river from Albany, Helen mentally wrote and rewrote a letter home.

You must understand—it's nothing to do with you. I love you both as much as ever, but the time has come for me to live my own life . . .

Three months later she was still trying to explain, but the letters ended up torn and crumpled in the metal wastebasket supplied by the Florence Nightingale Hotel for Women, where she now inhabited a small, spartan chamber on the fifteenth floor.

The family in St. Louis received from her postcards with views of the hotel and hastily written notes, jottings, for the most part, of where she had been and what she had seen. She went everywhere! Saw everything! And everything she saw excited and pleased her.

In spite of her lack of any kind of training or experience, she had found a job within a few weeks, and was supporting herself, through a series of coincidences that seemed to her, in her chronically febrile state, perfectly natural and ordinary happenings. A few days after her arrival in New York she had met a young woman in the hotel lobby by the name of Antoinette Wingover. Helen was standing at the desk, waiting for the clerk to finish sorting the afternoon mail, when the door of the telephone booth burst open and a rather stout, flushed girl, her arms full of books and packages, burst out, crying, "Now what am I supposed to do? Cut off by that stupid operator, and I'm utterly broke! Lend me a nickel, will you?"

Finding one in her change purse, Helen handed it over, and a few minutes later the girl reemerged. Unburdening herself onto one of the stiff lobby chairs, she brushed a lank strand of hair behind her ear with an impatient gesture and addressed Helen again. "Believe it or not, my roommate's gone off with the key, and I can't get into the apartment. She might not get home till midnight, and meanwhile I'm stuck."

Inside of fifteen minutes Helen had offered the use of her room as a place to leave the packages, lent her new acquaintance a dollar, and learned that Antoinette had lived in New York for a year, that she shared an apartment within walking distance of the hotel, and that she worked "in publishing."

"Well, actually, it's sort of a temporary job on an almanac," she explained. "My boss is an editor in the reference division – that's texts, not trade books – and he's hired a lot of people to work on this almanac. Are you looking for a job?"

She sounded tremendously experienced and knowledgeable to Helen, who had never contemplated the possibility of actually renting an apartment in New York. She admitted that she was looking for work.

"Have you a college degree?"

Her heart sinking, Helen had to admit she didn't.

"Well, that might not make any difference. Not many girls do . . . my boss might hire you just the same. Why don't you phone up for an appointment in the morning? Tell him I told you to call."

The Lesson of Tragedy

Near the end of her life, Helen thought, It seems odd, but it's true – some people have only one thing that ever happens to them, no matter how long they live, and everything gets built – accreted – around that one thing. Some people's lives are like that. In a way, they're the lucky ones, really—it makes their lives meaningful, there's a meaning in it for them. Not just a random series of events embedded in the gray clay of routine. Not just catastrophe, but Tragedy! With a capital T. Yes, she mused, What makes Tragedy is believing in it. The tragic hero or heroine is doomed, but since we're all doomed anyhow, maybe it's preferable to be a tragic hero. I couldn't do it, myself . . .

She suspected that, after all, Margaret Fuller had been wrong—when she said, Tragedy is always a mistake.

The Three Daughters

Once there were three daughters, Ethel, Helen, and Tessie. They lived with their parents in a big old house in St. Louis—it was before World War I—and they all thought about what they wanted to do when they grew up. Helen wanted to meet a lot of artists, and live in Italy, Ethel wanted to be a nurse, like Florence Nightingale, and Tessie wanted to have a big wedding with six bridesmaids all dressed in pink and carrying bouquets of tea roses.

Visiting the Sick

Ethel, taking a break from her volunteer work in the hospital library, is visiting Helen. She has brought a cardboard container of coffee.

Helen says, irritably, "You probably could have got some from the nurses' kitchenette—and in a real cup, too."

"It was only after I picked this up that I had the idea of stopping by to see you instead of going straight back to work."

The two sisters sit in silence.

"Do you remember Papa," says Helen after an interval. "After his operation–when he said he felt like the wonderful one-hoss shay in the poem, all coming to pieces at once–"

Ethel shoots Helen a glance suddenly shrewd. "Do you feel like that?"

"No, I was just thinking I don't. But what I do feel is that the parts are wearing out, one by one. And I don't want to have anything to do with it. It's as if I want to stay away from myself if I'm going to be sick, or old–is that possible? To be revolted by the signs of your own aging? And at the same time you feel a certain possessiveness about your own body, as if it's somehow to your credit for having stuck to it for such a long time. You even get fond of your own infirmities, as if they're marks of distinction."

Ethel says she has to leave now. In spite of having been herself a doctor, and the wife of a doctor in this very hospital for so many years, she feels uneasy in her sister's sickroom.

As for Helen, she is not sorry to see her sister go. Afterward, lying back against the pillows, it occurs to her that all the good works Ethel has done in the course of her long and active life require a certain insensitivity. "They call them Bleeding Hearts, but they're wrong. The Bleeding Hearts are the ones who can't bear even the sight of suffering, because seeing other people suffer makes them suffer so."

Philosophy

It never occurred to Ethel that everyone in the world didn't feel the same as she did, "deep down," or want the same things she did. She knew everyone didn't always think the same about everything – after all, there are Democrats and Republicans, Catholics and Protestants (even Jews and Muslims and all those others) – but weren't they all seeking God by different routes? Everyone knows Communism is the same as a religion.

"Even atheists are deeply religious," she used to say, with a very serious expression, as if her seriousness clinched the argument.

Is Helen a Virgin?

No, Helen isn't a virgin. The family in St. Louis knew nothing about it, but in the years between twenty-five and forty-five she had four lovers, although she never married. The most important, to her, was Wolf Tombey, the alcoholic poet whose spectacular suicide in Times Square shortly before Pearl Harbor has already become myth.

Now that she is a spinster, close to seventy, does it make any difference? What can the world say, looking at her? Only that she has a history. Something has happened. She herself, now that she no longer thinks of those men except as she thinks of her own long-ago self – thinks that they simply represent her accessibility to experience.

II

The New Madrid earthquake began without warning, early in the morning of December 16, 1811. Because, outside of the towns of New Madrid (pop. about 200 families) and Caruthersville (about 100 families), the area was largely wilderness, the quake did not attract much attention, either at the time or later. Nevertheless, it produced significant changes in the geography of the area. River banks caved in, new lakes were created, islands disappeared, and the course of the mighty Mississippi was altered.

Justice

"It's the wrong place to look for justice, the universe," Helen thinks. She thinks of Wolf, his work forgotten after the brief flurry of notoriety that followed his spectacular suicide. She recalls her brother-in-law Ralph's death, Hobart's wife's accident, her own mother's long invalidism and decay into senility, the boy crushed in the driveway under the wheels of his own father's car, rat poison put out by mistake and eaten by a dog, the thalidomide babies, the assassinations, the one child out of seven who didn't escape from the burning house, all the black pages of history, the plague, concentration camps, Hiroshima, Biafra, Vietnam.

"The first thing I thought of – when I was a child and they told me the story of Noah's Ark – was, what about the *other animals?* They weren't bad – but he only took two. Why couldn't they all be saved? Springeth up – and is cut down. Is there justice for one grass blade, as against another?"

The History of Rasselas

Meeting Anders Durk for the first time at 8:00 A.M. in the deserted publisher's office, Helen was not in any way intimidated, since she had no expectation of getting the job. Stepping out of the elevator into the reception room, she was pleasantly impressed by the bookish, book-lined walls and leather settees (it was only later she learned that the books were dummies and the leather imitation). No receptionist sat at the polished cherrywood desk; none of the staff were due to arrive until nine. Helen stood indecisively for what could have been no more than a few seconds when a door on the right opened and an enormous man peered out. This was Anders Durk. He stood six feet three inches tall, but his burly shoulders and huge girth made him seem far larger. Even his face was outsized, and his eyes—oddly dreamy and mild—were magnified by the thick, steel-rimmed lenses he wore.

"Miss Houser," he said, and led her through a big, slovenly room filled with a maze of desks, chairs, and filing cabinets to a cubicle in which he motioned her to take a seat. He then lowered himself into a chair behind his own desk, on which books and papers were spread out in confusion.

"So you think you would like to work here," he mused. "Tell me something about yourself, Miss Houser."

"I hardly know where to begin," Helen began.

Anders Durk interrupted her. "Are you familiar with these sentiments?" He started to read, in his big, booming voice, from one of the books open on his table. "Ye who listen with credulity to the whispers of fancy, and pursue with eagerness the phantoms of hope; who expect that age will perform the promise of youth, and that the deficiencies of the present day will be supplied by the morrow; attend to the history of Rasselas, prince of Abyssinia . . ."

"That's Dr. Johnson, isn't it?" Helen asked.

"Yes, yes," said Durk. "What's he talking about?"

"He might as well be talking about anyone who's optimistic about the future of society today," said Helen slowly. "I suppose he meant the optimists, or liberals, of his own time."

"I suppose so," rumbled the big man. "You do some reading, I see, Miss Houser. Tell me, have you a favorite modern author?"

Helen thought the question odd, since, from what Antoinette had told her about the job, it had nothing to do with literature, but she was almost enjoying herself. For the next few minutes they discussed "modern authors," while she became aware that the big office outside his cubicle was beginning to fill. Drawers opened and shut, chairs were pushed back, coat hangers jangled, and voices, even laughter, were heard.

Finally Durk said, "I'll settle the pay with the front office, then. You know it won't be high. This isn't a high-paying business. You can come in next week. Monday. Start Monday, nine o'clock." He turned entirely businesslike. "The hours are nine until six, lunch from twelve to one, half a day on Saturdays."

She left elated. It was a feeling that never wholly left her, during all the years she worked for Anders Durk. It had to do with independence, with freedom, with being part of the crowd in the packed elevators, part of the crowds in the hurrying New York streets.

Introducing Wolf

Wolf Tombey, the doomed, drunken poet destined to become, briefly, a legend when he killed himself in Times Square shortly before Pearl Harbor, was hired by Anders Durk about a year after Helen went to work at the almanac. He did not stay long, but it was long enough to change Helen's life.

Hobart's Life

To the women in it, chiefly, at this time, Louise, Vera, and Binnie, Hobart's life is entirely opaque. Even by the most enormous effort of will, Louise can't imagine what it would be like to *be* Hobart. *Being Hobart.* She is probably, of all people on earth, the one closest to him, the one who knows most "about" him. She knows his family background, his home town, the house, even the room, where he grew up, his parents, his brothers, and how he happened to become a doctor. Although when she heard that story it shocked her so profoundly, wounding her in the most vulnerable part of her romantic sensibility, that in her very rare introspective moments she has suspected herself of marrying him precisely on that account.

It's a straightforward story. The second of four brothers, Hobart had wanted to study engineering, but his older brother was already an engineer, and the parents had decided their second son was to be a doctor.

"You didn't dream of helping humanity – as a boy – you didn't imagine yourself healing the sick, alleviating suffering?"

"Not really," an amused Hobart had replied to a much-younger, near-febrile Louise. "Only the way all kids do, I guess – didn't you? My mother wanted to have a doctor for a son – maybe *she* thought about it like that. And it's a good income. I knew I was smart enough to get through medical school without any trouble, so that was how I happened to decide on medicine."

"But you're a *good* doctor."

"Of course I am."

She had seen him in her mind's eye, tall, white-coated, cold as ice, striding down hospital corridors, an animated instrument of healing. More than anyone she had ever known, he was The Other. No one could possibly be more different from herself. His rejection of her romantic image of him only made him, to her infatuated eyes, in her overheated imagination, more romantic.

Besides, his lovemaking excited her. She had had other lovers, but what gave her a secret, voluptuous thrill was her own vision, in the midst of his flushed and fumbling fondlings, limbs hot and damp intertwined, of the ice-hard, abstract core that she sensed at his center: implacable, invincible, scientific.

And so they were married.

Will She Live?

Louise is furious with her surgeon. She rages, "I told him, 'All I want to know is, will I live or die?' And he – that conceited ape – he said to me, 'That isn't what you want me to tell you – you're smart enough to know that everybody's going to die sooner or later. You're asking me to be something I'm not – you want me to be God.' – God!" she explodes, "it's nothing to do with God – or with him, either – it has to do with *me, me, me!*"

The sound, three times repeated, hangs in the air, a

hoarse, plaintive cry. Does Louise herself hear it, lingering there?

Hobart has a sudden, involuntary view of the sound waves it has created, diminishing ripples, spreading out into the vast, indifferent silence.

Years of Savagery

transmittable
issue in
objects
coded
life filling the screen as a
loosen, disunite
object-oriented thing
fills a bathtub simultaneously filling and emptying
a vision or, if you prefer
this neurosis
at the same rate
FEROCITY OF PUR-POSE
Note form or
at the site, clotted
scratched
clawed
hatched
drugged
dragged
CANONS OF
plexiglass forms, filled
dabbed
scored

scarred, worried, obsolescent, or

piles of

dirt

A tub of water, and

troubled/untroubled pools

SUCCESS OVERTOOK HIM

'Art does not necessarily

brute/complex

produce /police

input, or

feed, if you prefer

forty minutes on the telephone

—optional!

listening to each other breathe,

for God's sake!

irreducible presence

A Likeness

Edmund has the scruffy, limp brown hair lying close to his skull, beginning to grow over his collar, and the polite, attentive look, the appearance of being perpetually poised on the edge of his chair, of the middle-aged boy; a network of tiny, fine wrinkles overlays the boyish profile. His eyes have that limpid, liquid look that comes only with contact lenses.

The women and girls who make up the majority of his patients find his boyish looks exceedingly romantic. The younger and more literary ones can picture him in a velvet jacket and flowing bohemian tie, looking rather like de Musset in an old engraving. Rumors about his heavy drinking and exotic sexual preferences add, if anything, to his fascination for them, especially since in his actual presence they find it difficult to credit him with any but the most poetic and spiritual desires.

Edmund himself, entirely aware of the reactions he provokes, is alternately entertained and disgusted by them. To Vera, he says, "Darling old cows, they'll make me rich."

He has come calling, with one of his wonderfully distracting gifts, in the long afternoon while Louise marks time waiting for Hobart to come back from the hospital. He sits on her waiting sofa.

"Being both fish and fowl," he has told her gravely, "who better than I can *tout comprendre, tout pardonner?* With one foot (you'll pardon the expression) in either camp, I'm equipped to understand both you and the doctors."

He is a plastic surgeon, one of the best in the country.

"There are plenty of sculptors now who don't do their own actual assembling—some of them don't even make working drawings or models. Look at Mark di Suvero, right here in St. Louis—since his accident he can't build those big things himself! He works with wood and metal, fastened together with wire and stuff, but now that he's crippled, he can't climb around on them to fasten the parts together, so he has some guys working for him. He just tells them where to put it, and they put it there," says Edmund.

Louise won't meet his eyes. She runs her finger around and around the rim of her highball glass.

"But doesn't he miss handling the material?"

"It's a different experience, that's all."

Rich's Cold

Rich, who has been out of town at a convention for three days, has a cold. His eyes are watery, his nose is red, his throat is full of phlegm, and he is not interested in making love. "For God's sake, Binnie, I feel awful," he says, shaking off her solicitous hand on his brow. "I never should have come."

"You might just as well feel miserable here as all alone in that empty house," says Binnie. Rich's wife Corinne and the children are at her mother's for one more week before she takes up her conjugal responsibilities once more. "Would you like to go to bed?"

"Where would you sleep, if I did?" he growls. "I certainly don't want you coming near me. You'd be sure to catch it."

"I'll make you a hot toddy," she says hopefully.

"Hell, no, I'm going home to my own bed. I really shouldn't have come. I'll phone you in a day or two—don't call me; Corinne may be back," says Rich, winding his woollen muffler around his throat and shrugging his way into his overcoat. "No, no, don't kiss me, and don't come to the door—stay as far away as you can."

At the apartment door he manages a grin and waves two fingers, crookedly, at her. "So long, sweetie. I'll be seeing you."

Cultivates

the accidental
anti-permanent
transmutation of form and content
creative
totemistic
primordial domains
antipodal
flattened and perforated surfaces

ABOLISHES IDENTITY

mesmeric iconography

calligraphic bimorphic

anti-dimensional

logical

cellular

vertical/horizontal

FREEZES TENDERNESS

the apotheosis of the banal

reactivation of the

ominous

mass

organic petrifaction

baroque petrifaction

compartmentalized

CALIBRATES THE NEGATIVE

constructual

phantoms of technology hybrid allusions

manipulates reality

Inside a Matchbox

Edmund told Louise that during the war Giacometti started making such tiny figures that his entire *oeuvre* for those years could fit inside a matchbox.

Edmund said, "He did it not because wartime conditions prevented him from working on anything bigger, but because he became interested in the problem of how to make figures that would look as if you were seeing them from a great distance, even when they were actually up close."

Louise did not say anything at the time, but her eyes took on a glazed, inward look. She lit a cigarette.

The Medium

"Some of that stuff–it's toxic. Like plastic wood–it gets absorbed through the pores and rots the brain. Take what happened to Mallary. He was using this spray, see, and he started getting headaches. Then nausea–vomiting–they didn't know what it was. So then when he had to quit working for a while, he got better . . . And when he started to work again, the headaches and vomiting started all over again. He was breathing it in, see, the spray. His own work was killing him."

Largest Known Displacement

brought up to admire and trust in the police, like we were
OCCURRED IN 1899 AT YAKUTAT BAY,
ALASKA
when the dust began to settle and people began to
crawl about in the wreckage
saw his back arch as the shot hit
just like Vietnam
THE GROUND ROSE AND FELL LIKE THE LONG LOW SWELL
OF
THE SEA
"You can't do anything about a natural disaster," he said
"Unlike pollution and other
AREAS SANK
earlier attacks on folk songs and the graduated income tax
we never believed they'd
really start shooting us."
WHOLE ISLANDS DISAPPEARED
stabbed, bitten, shot, subjected to electric shocks, thrown
violently to the floor, hit with fists, kicked,

stamped on, burned with open
flames
COUNTED AS AUTOBIOGRAPHICAL FRAGMENTS
from lighted cigarettes, electric irons, and hot pokers
beaten with rubber
EARTHQUAKE INSURANCE AVAILABLE
hoses, broom handles, and baseball bats
IS IT A COINCIDENCE ?
turned its weapons of
war on its own children and has gunned them down and then

In what classrooms do they teach the children the history of the hundreds of earthquakes, some tiny and some immense, that have shaken the North American continent in the more than 200 years since the foundation of the Republic? Even earlier, between 1628 and 1782, over a hundred and fifty severe shocks are reported to have occurred. Almost a quarter of a century before the Declaration of Independence, a violent tremor set all Boston trembling, alarming many, who took it as an intimation of doom, and sent them gibbering to the churches in desperate, last-minute attempts to atone for real or imagined sins.

Her Life Is Over

Ethel can't believe her life with Ralph is over. "So quickly!" she mourns, shaking her head in disbelief at the notion that they were married for more than forty years. "A lifetime, you might say . . . but I can remember the day we were married as if it were yesterday, such a bright, cold morning, running out to the Chinese laundry to pick up Ralph's clean shirts so he could pack for going away, the trip to Mackinac Island, that enormous hotel . . . we wondered if they knew we were on our honeymoon. You know, Helen, it does seem as if it's all been downhill since then, when everything was just beginning, all of us so hopeful, the war over and the world ready to listen to reason, President Wilson someone you could really look up to—but after that, Harding . . . and then to have our own boys accuse us, blaming us for Mussolini and Hitler, the sharecroppers under Roosevelt, concentration camps, as if it had been our fault! But didn't we do what we could? All our life together, I thought we were succeeding. I really believed it . . . and now, nothing left . . . nobody left . . . only you and poor Tessie to remember Ralph and the way it really was."

Silently, Helen pats her arm. Catching herself with wet eyes, Ethel wipes them fiercely and gets up to go. "What a complaining old lady I'm getting to be," she says, resettling her glasses on her reddened nose.

Rich's Wife

Binnie can't imagine what Corinne is like—what it would be like to be Corinne. She has seen her once or twice at a distance, a slender figure in a fur-collared coat, a neat profile at the wheel of Rich's Mercedes—once, even, at a party, the one where she first met Rich, shortly before Corinne became ill and went away.

Binnie Waits

One day, waiting for Rich outside the hospital, Binnie thinks about her colleagues, "We're all displaced persons in a sense, even if Vera is the only one who has actually physically left her own country . . . Ethel, alone in a strange place, trying to learn how to live without Uncle Ralph; Edmund, of course . . . Hobart I don't really know about, but his wife's an artist, that places her . . . God knows how I fit into my own category. I really don't belong in this hole-and-corner business, hanging around outside the institution of marriage like a beggar . . . Rich and Corinne . . ." But she doesn't like to think about Rich's wife. Usually she can avoid it, since they never meet, but now that Corinne is about to come back to St. Louis, Binnie finds that the idea of her is intruding more and more. It's as though her physical proximity—to what?—to Rich?—clothes her abstract self, the depersonalized concept of "Rich's wife" with a disquieting solidity. He doesn't ("Thank God!" Binnie had said to her friend Sarah months before, before anything had really "happened") keep a picture of his wife on his desk, although since the end of November there has appeared a studio portrait of the two children, emerging side by side from sepia shadows. Binnie hasn't mentioned it, and Rich has said nothing about it either.

Ethel's Discovery

Ethel is entirely serious about her suggestion that the hospital refuse to accept any indigent or needy patients. "You know, I never realized it before," she told Grace and Binnie, "but they actually lose money on every one! Medicare and Medicaid don't begin to cover costs on those patients! Why, I had no idea! I used to order all the tests when one of them came in, even though they might not all have been really necessary, you know, but just in case—and anyway, they don't have to pay for them, do they? But Dr. Semple was just telling me that the hospital gets only a fixed fee, it's something like $3.50, for each one of these people! And when you put that up against rising costs, lab fees, technician's salaries, nurses, equipment—it's a joke. It isn't even a drop in the bucket!" She said indignantly, "I told him, 'These people are *destroying* the hospital.'"

She is shocked right down to the very center of her being. "But he said they can't give up the clinic patients. The hospital needs them for the students." She sighed. "And besides, he said it would be bad for The Image."

Listening, aghast, Binnie was just about to say something when Grace burst out, "But doesn't the hospital exist in order to help people? I mean, especially those people, Aunt Ethel, the ones who can't pay? After all, what's the hospital *for?*"

But Ethel could only distractedly repeat, "They are destroying the hospital!"

The New Madrid earthquake of 1811 exceeded in severity any recorded earthquake in the history of the North American continent, including the San Francisco earthquake of 1906 and the Alaska earthquake of 1964.

The number of shocks, the persistence of the disturbance (it continued for more than a year), the area affected, and the severity of the sequence all combined to make it a major geological disturbance. The surface geology and topography of the region suggest earthquake activity of significant magnitude over the past several thousand years, and mild earthquake activity continues there today; approximately 100 earthquakes have been recorded in the Illinois-Missouri area since 1811.

Only the fact that the surrounding territory was largely unpopulated at the time prevented it from being a major disaster. If an earthquake were to occur in the same area today, it would cause hundreds of thousands of dollars worth of property damage as far away as St. Louis, and undoubtedly result in considerable loss of life.

The elastic-rebound theory of earthquakes postulates that rocks are elastic and that mechanical energy is stored in them as it is in a compressed spring. When slippage occurs along a fault in the earth's crust, some of the frictional stress the rocks exerted on each other is violently released, and the rocks along the fault spring back to equilibrium. This springing back, or rebound, may take place in a matter of seconds – resulting in an earthquake – or it may take days, or even years, in which case the seismic energy radiated at any given moment is so small as to be almost unnoticeable.

Changes

Tess remarks to Helen, with a worried look, that Ethel is beginning to let herself go. She still takes pains with her appearance when she comes over to the hospital or goes to a meeting of one of her committees, but at home the first telltale signs have begun to appear. She spends whole days shuffling around the apartment in dilapidated satin mules, uncorseted under her brunch coat, its bosom spotted with tiny flecks of egg and grease.

"I don't even know where she got those terrible slippers," says Tess, "I don't ever remember seeing them before."

Helen says, "Maybe her eyes are getting bad. You ought to suggest that she see an eye man."

Wolf's Stigmata

Sober, Wolf was a rather small, soft-spoken man whose slight appearance belied a sinewy strength. His hair, worn longer than the current mode, was dark and fine; he combed it down with brilliantine. He wore dark glasses, and sported a long, silky moustache in the style of E. A. Poe; the tips of his two middle fingers on his left hand were badly mangled, having been (as he later told Helen) caught in a threshing machine on the Kansas farm from which he had escaped, like a prisoner fleeing from a cell, some fifteen years earlier. When he had been drinking, "My stigmata," he would explain, thrusting the mutilated hand into some young woman's fascinated face. Until his first paycheck he worked industriously at the desk assigned to him, never speaking to any of his colleagues, seldom lifting his eyes from the papers in front of him.

As Helen later discovered, he had been almost literally starving during that first month. The arrival of his first check happened to coincide with a particularly upsetting letter from his mother, who was demanding that he return to Kansas City, where she now lived; and the combination of having some money in his pocket, food in his stomach, and a good excuse in the letter made it inevitable that he would go on a spree.

Showing up in the office the next day at noon, he lurched through the door, tousled, reeking of alcohol, in the same clothing he had worn the day before, now crumpled, stained, and dusty, and slammed into his chair, where he remained for the rest of the day, groaning loudly at intervals and holding his head between his hands. It was impossible to ignore him, although the typists and female editorial assistants (of whom Helen was one) went out of their way to avoid the region of his desk.

The following day he appeared at the regular time, behaving with his usual circumspection. Nothing remained of his previous day's condition except a black eye that not even his dark glasses could conceal.

Hobart Has Not Changed

"Hobart hasn't changed, nothing could ever possibly change him," Louise states with conviction. "I used to think that just being made Division Chief changed people. I remember what happened to Ralph—not that I didn't love him, you know I did. But nobody could deny there was a *change* in him. I mean, he was *different*. But not Hobart. He's exactly the same as always."

"Yes, I think you are probably right," Vera agrees. She sits on the edge of a chair in Louise's living room, trying not to look at her watch; she has allotted fifteen minutes to this visit, but doesn't want Louise to suspect she has been scheduled in. "You know him better, of course, than any of us. You know if he has changed."

"Not Hobart," Louise reiterates. But she has lost interest in the conversation. The truth of the matter is that she has never spent any time at the hospital, and has no idea of what Hobart is like there, or what his life there is like. She still tends to envisage it, when she thinks of it at all, like a set of stills out of some dimly remembered movie. Dedicated faces are bent over an anesthetized form supine on a table. Skilled hands are adjusting a needle for intravenous transfusion, or holding a test tube to the light: "Just as we feared, it is the deadly plague bacillus, unknown on this continent for nearly a hundred years." Not even a soap opera would dare to be as corny as these images. "Doctor, a fine baby boy."

Has Nothing Changed?

When Helen came back to St. Louis after twenty-five years it was as though she had never gone away. There were changes, of course; her father had died, her nephews grown up, her baby sister become a grandmother. But the ladies who came to visit Mom-mom as she lay in bed throughout her last long illness, even Ethel and Tessie, hardly seemed aware of the fact that there had been a time when she, Helen, had not been there with them, sharing all their concerns.

She thought of the knight in the fairy tale, lured by an elf-woman through the magic door in the mountain, where he stayed all night, only to find, when he awoke next morning on the bare hillside, that he was an old man with his whole life gone.

Sometimes she wondered whether she had ever really gone away. Once, fastening an earring that Wolf had given her, in front of the big old-fashioned mirror in the big old-fashioned bedroom that is hers once more, she said aloud, "But things *have* happened."

Helen and Wolf

In the first flush of their love for each other, Wolf gave up his furnished room and moved into Helen's apartment on Charles Street, but it did not take long for them to find out that it was impossible for them to live together.

My darling, he wrote to her from Key West, where he had fled from the domesticity that quickly became intolerable to him, *there is nothing I long for more than to be with you—in every sense—for ever and ever. How is it that this cannot be? What is it, in us two, that drives us apart as surely and as strongly as, when we are apart, it pulls us together? . . .*

After a week or two he returned to the city without telling Helen, and took a room on West Fourth Street. She didn't know he was back, until one evening on her way home from work she stopped at the little grocery store on the corner to get something for her solitary dinner, and they found themselves face to face over a pyramid of Rinso boxes. Speechless, they walked through the mild light of a May evening to his basement quarters.

Following that first electric reunion, she would sometimes come and clean for him, collect his soiled shirts and take them to the laundry. More often than not, he ate dinner in her apartment, or they both went down the street to Chumley's or the Blue Boar, where Wolf was in his element among the writers and painters who had crowded into the Village during the twenties and remained there during the thirties.

Ups and Downs

Helen, now working for a different publisher, was very happy when Wolf was writing, in spite of the many evenings she was all alone. She felt herself rewarded by finding in her mailbox, when she returned from work, a draft of a new poem or a revision of an old one – sometimes only a fragment, a line or two, or an extended passage of the long poem that was taking most of his energy.

She could always tell when he had had a letter from home, for that was enough to trigger his wildest excesses. He would start drinking in the morning, right after the mail was delivered, and by the time she got home at six o'clock anything might have happened. The telephone bell ringing in her silent apartment signalled disaster.

"Christ, darling, I'm in the police station, don't ask me how I got here. First thing I know I'm playing with somebody's lost poodle. The cop who pulled me in tells me he asked me what I was doing and I told him it was none of his goddamn business . . . I outsmarted him, though; on the way here in the car I threw all my identification out the window . . . luckily I didn't have any dough or that would have gone too. But anyway, can you get right over here and tell them who the hell I am?"

Love Betrayed

Rich has told Binnie now that Corinne is back he thinks they shouldn't see each other any more.

Just like a torch song, she thinks: It's over. She is surprised to find her eyes swimming with tears.

"The trouble is," Binnie tells herself, "I agree with him. I think he's absolutely right." She knows she never should have had anything to do with him in the first place. "A married man with two children—and a sick wife—what kind of a bitch would—?"

She knew it all along.

But now what is she to do?

No matter how hard she rubs them, sitting at her office desk, her eyes keep overflowing with tears. "Idiot!" she tells herself, "Your eyes'll get swollen, your nose'll get red—suppose someone comes in?"

But she can't stop.

"Think about something else, the really bad things, all the injustice in the world, people starving, useful causes. Too ridiculous, a smart girl like you . . . attractive, too . . . much too old for this sort of thing . . ."

She will immerse herself in her work.

She will go to Europe.

She'll leave St. Louis . . . she'll stay in St. Louis . . . she'll show him. She'll find another man. "What kind of a bitch—?"

"At least I'm not pregnant," she tells herself, sniffling violently, scrubbing her nose with a sodden Kleenex. "I wish I were."

The tears continue to well out of her eyes, running down her cheeks, dripping humiliatingly off her chin.

The only known injury resulting from the recent earthquake in the Rockies, which shook an area of approximately 400 square miles and registered 6.3 on the Richter scale, was a cut on the leg inflicted by falling stage scenery, reported by a girl at a rehearsal in Malad City, Idaho. In Salt Lake City, Utah, spectators at a dance performance demanded their money back because they said the entire balcony was shaking. The audience watching the movie, *Earthquake,* experiencing the real thing, assumed it was part of the special effects.

III

The Family Photographs

Here in a shoebox is a collection of snapshots of Ethel and Ralph. The earliest ones, in which the costumes look impossibly old-fashioned, are mostly group pictures of gawky young men in shirtsleeves or shawl-necked sweaters, girls in ankle-length plaid skirts, rapidly succeeded by the dashing bobs and knees of the succeeding period. Many seem to have been taken on beaches. The next series omits both Ralph and Ethel and displays, instead, one or more of the little boys. Next, class pictures, camp pictures, autographed pictures of the cast of a high school play. Passing rapidly over the ones of her cousins, Binnie pauses at one of her Uncle Ralph looking hale and ruddy in a V-necked sweater and flannel slacks; this is the way she remembers him from the visits of her childhood – not in his hospital whites, but tweedy, relaxed, expansive. Aunt Ethel, a slight frown wrinkling her rounded forehead above the pink shell-rimmed glasses she used to wear, is at his side; their arms are linked against a background of autumn foliage.

"Let's see, that must have been taken about fifteen years ago," Ethel says, the same frown that appears in the photo creasing her brow as she peers nearsightedly over Binnie's shoulder. "Doesn't Ralph look wonderful there? He was never sick a day in his life, a remarkable constitution, you know!"

The Generation Gap / 2

When they show Ethel Bertrand Russell's letter to the American editor in which he says that he owes his happiness to his invariable habit of defecating twice every day, she nods approvingly.

Susie and her boyfriend explode into laughter. "But, Auntie, don't you see—it was his way of saying what he thinks of the editor for asking him such a stupid question," Susie explains to her great-aunt.

Ethel is unconvinced. "I don't know about the editor, but I do know both your Great-Uncle Ralph and I always believed in the importance of regular bowel habits for a sense of well-being."

Is it possible that the earthquakes at New Madrid, Missouri never occurred at all? In 1883 one James MacFarlane published a paper denying that there had ever been any earthquake activity in the area. He argued that the "sunk lands" of Tennessee, Missouri, and Arkansas, and particularly Reelfoot Lake, generally believed to have been created by that series of violent earth tremors, had come into being, instead, as a result of the gradual dissolution of the limestone understrata, followed by the collapse of the surface.

What Happens

Sue said to Binnie, "But what if nothing ever happens?"

Binnie answered obliquely, "Andy Warhol said, 'I like boring things.'"

"But he's such a phony."

Binnie and Hobart

Briefly alone, behind the bulwark of her desk in the tastefully decorated office on the hospital's main floor, Binnie thinks, "The reprehensible fact: the longer Louise is laid up, and the longer, consequently, Hobart is under this deadly strain, the more out of sympathy with him I feel."

She finds herself accumulating grievances, adding up all the things Hobart has ever done that she didn't like. "His tired old World War II anecdotes, and all that jungle rot," she says to herself derisively. His repudiation of Edmund. His toadying to Trudman, the new pathologist—not calling on him to do anything, while the others do all the work that piled up while they were looking for someone. —And Hobart took his time over that, too! Then—telling everyone how brilliant Trudman is, finding him an apartment, going out of his way to show him around town—just because he's black, that's all. Showing everyone how goddamn broad-minded he is. And his support of Semple! A man everyone knows is an anti-Semite and a racist. It occurs to her that it's possible he backs Semple because that's a way of expressing his own hostilities, while on the surface he goes on hiring people like Edmund and Derek Trudman. Weren't there rumors on the staff—"Hobart's afraid of pushy New York Jews," "Hobart's afraid of Derek"?

Art and Life

"Sometimes I really worry about Louise," Hobart tells Vera. "She never used to talk like that. Yesterday she said she didn't see any point in knocking herself out when all she'd be doing is making new junk out of old junk."

He paused expectantly. "She was looking at the latest copy of *Art News*."

Vera says, "Yes, it is difficult for you, especially since you have not been used to this. But I must tell you, Hobart, many artists talk this way all the time—but this does not prevent them from making their 'junk.'" She smiles.

"You don't understand. She really meant it—that it was—

is – nothing but junk. Art. She said she wonders how grown men and women can justify spending their whole lives at it. She said she thinks that art is nothing but an evasion of responsibility, human responsibility. Louise never talked like that before."

"Yes, well, she can always go to the Social Work School," says Vera calmly. "It will keep her busy, and nobody objects if a social worker has only one leg. But I do not think she will do this."

Wild Predictions

I don't know how we got into
the war but one of the problems
now is civil rights for the
DISASTROUS EARTHQUAKES
emphasized the divinity of
Christ, appealed for stoical acceptance
of death on the battlefield, and quoted
Sherwood Anderson, Joan of Arc,
and Shakespeare
NOT SUPPORTED
so tormented she tried to commit suicide
by putting her head in the toilet and
flushing it NO MORE PREDICTABLE
comes as naturally to male and female
as breathing, loving, hating, laughing,
FRIGHTENING MANY
crying, or any other emotion
not transmitted through the core, and
others holding that they do struggle through but
with little energy remaining
LITTLE SOLACE IN PHILOSOPHY

ALMOST REFRESHING *theoretically completed in 305*
days, whereas actually

there is no more soul in a heart than
in a slice of calf's liver

A MAJOR FAULT

"I'll have to investigate further to see just what
hero-type actions they performed," said
the senator.

Hobart's Dilemma

Edmund said to Binnie, "I see that Hobart is managing to get along in spite of his wife's difficulties."

"What does that mean?" says Binnie; she is offended.

"Isn't he finding new ways to get his kicks? He *ogles,* for one thing. He never used to ogle. And haven't you seen him pinching the nurses and patting the secretaries?"

"Edmund, you are impossible. I haven't, and neither have you." But she feels uneasy.

"If you really haven't, keep your eyes open, love," says Edmund, and vanishes into his own office with a lewd wink.

What They Are Getting Into

Grace thought, "They don't have the faintest notion of what they're getting into."

Aloud she said to Sue and her boyfriend, "You kids do not realize what you're getting into."

The trouble is, she went on in her own mind, you can't know until you're in it. Her own twenty-year-old self isn't so far away that she can't summon it back sometimes: the months right after Susie was born, living all alone with her in a furnished room—they called it an apartment. It had a hot plate in a closet and a refrigerator out on the landing, which she shared with the two other tenants (also army wives), along with the single bathroom. Its only advantage was that it was near the army camp where Walter was stationed for basic training. She finds nothing in her mind to bring back the reality of the town where they were living, but only—and that very vividly—("and I haven't thought of it for years," she thinks, with some surprise) her intense physical relationship with the baby. Waking in the hot bright mornings to Susie's first chirpings, stumbling to lift her from the portable crib and then lying next to her, both of them half-stupefied in the sour-sweet smell of milk, urine, her own sweat, and Johnson's baby powder. Later she might bathe and change, first herself and then the baby, and they would go out to the grocery store, or down to where a little bridge crossed the slow, dazzling creek that meandered through this end of town; but for the most part what she remembers is lying on the bed with Susie, eating oranges and cookies and drinking milk, now and then turning the pages of a magazine. The baby waves her toes in the air, clutches at her mother's tousled hair and tugs, and Grace—the twenty-year-old Grace—buries her face in her daughter's fat stomach and they are both laughhg.

The doctor had said "No chocolate cookies—" no good for the milk. Why should she sleep through the night and be awake in the daytime? "It's just an arbitrary schedule —" So—for how many months?—Grace lived on the baby's schedule, sleeping and waking and eating when the baby did. The only times it inconvenienced her were when Walter had a weekend pass and came into town, but there was always someone to leave the baby with. One of the other young wives was always happy to take her. Grace would fix her hair, do her nails, climb into a dress, and leave the howling baby in one of the other apartments without a backward look, and she and Walter would go dancing, dancing, wrapped in each other's arms in a kind of swoon, until it was time for him to hurry back to the camp.

And all the while, Tessie had been after her to come home with the baby and move in with her until Walter's army service was over. Especially before the baby was born, she had been insistent on the long-distance telephone. "–All that way off, and you don't know what kind of a place it will be and who the doctors are–while here you have such a fine hospital and your uncle can see to it that you have the best of care."

Grace had said, "Oh, *Mother*."

"That's all very well, you feel fine and I'm delighted, but you kids don't know what can *happen*, not that I want to alarm you, of course–"

And then, after Susie's birth, "You know I'm not the kind of person to feel sorry for myself, but isn't it natural to want to see my first grandchild? I can't wait to hug her," she had written, her curiously unformed handwriting dipping and soaring on the page. "I can remember the first time I held you in my arms–of course things were different then–your father never would have permitted me to come home without a nurse. Her name was Mrs. Bannister, and she was a real tyrant; I was afraid to say Boo! She stayed and took care of you for two weeks after we came home, and of course in those days we stayed in the hospital for two weeks at least–nothing like now; I don't know how you girls do it. You can't imagine how nervous I was when Mrs. B finally left and I had to give you a bath for the first time all by myself–I was so afraid I'd drop you, or you'd drown, or both! But I phoned up Ethel, and she came right over and helped."

Grace is far more tolerant of her mother now than she had been all those years ago when she received that letter; she thinks, "Even after all these years, Mother still hasn't changed; now she's carrying on about Sue," but the emotion she feels isn't the old mixture of impatience and irritation; it is something very much like love.

Investigators

beginning with Love have found
in the future
waiting in vain
wretched hundreds
toiling away at the enormous
SHADOW ZONE
due to a gradual contraction of the earth's surface
a crumbling and a cracking up
of the globe
reaching instantly to the earth's
upper caverns, and
explode!
One paper was visible on top of
the pile. It said, "No."
DOMINATING LINK
Something is happening here and we don't know what it is,
he said in unconscious parody
and toward such mediocrity aspired!
(Of course, this statement cannot be proved, but probably it
is *nearer to the truth than is generally recognized.)*

Many within the New Madrid earthquake area started to count the tremors, but only Jared Brooks persevered in keeping count. By rigging both pendulums capable of detecting horizontal movement, and springs that indicated vertical movement, he recorded a total of one thousand, eight hundred and seventy-four separate shocks between December 16, 1811, and March 15, 1812.

Louise Has Not Changed

Louise has never been introspective. Before the accident, she had been accustomed to translate her feelings and thoughts more or less directly into sculptural forms. She chipped stone, gouged wood, bent and twisted metal, wrestled and hoisted the raw materials of her vision into shapes expressive and plastic without any need to bypass direct action by means of words.

Since the accident, she has not changed. All that has changed is her ability to lift, shove, pull, push, cut, polish, and force the unwieldy mass of her materials into the semblance of harmony she craves. She sits in her padded chair and doodles. At the end of the endless day she tears off the sullied sheets and crumples them into the wastebasket.

"It's no use fishing them out of there," she says sharply to Vera. "This is not a low-budget movie."

Vera is abashed, but only momentarily. From now on she takes the basket into the kitchen out of Louise's sight, before removing the sketches, which she carefully smooths out and places in a portfolio. But in spite of her conscientious husbanding of the creative impulse, Vera is wrong, and Louise is right. The sketches are useless, dead, and without value.

In a rare moment of self-analysis, Louise remarks, "I'm like old Alice the elephant, the star of the elephant show at the zoo. I saw her last year, poor thing, covered with ulcerated sores and dying – poor mad thing, she was chained by one leg and still dancing obsessively on and on, red-eyed, her poor trunk bobbing and swaying – "

She snorts, and crushes another drawing in her strong, oddly masculine sculptor's hands.

Trudman Takes Charge

"They've got the new pathologist, Trudman, in charge at the lab," Binnie tells her friend Sarah.

"Married?"

"No. But he's black – and beautiful."

The Troublemaker

Edmund told Binnie it was the moving-in of the Jewish Mafia that had brought about the decline and fall of Gaslight Square, that artificial pleasure zone of cafes, restaurants, and bars that flourished briefly in the crook of the city's elbow. "You don't know about the Jewish Mafia? The real bigtime's up in Chicago, but these guys moved in from K.C. They set up their hookers and pushers, or took over the ones that were already here – you remember the Boboli Gardens, that place with the tables in the courtyard – and the Grinning Ape, and Elfie's, and the Cafe Pernod? They ran them all . . . I know a chick used to work out of there – a hooker. She told me all about it. Double protection, she was paying – to the fuzz and the J.M. – And I'll tell you something else you don't know. Up on De Baliviere, along there between Lindell and Delmar, where all those bars are – that's where they recruit young boys. They'll either grab them—or they'll coax them—but once they go with those guys, that's it. They don't have a chance. There's a known clientele for those boys. Supply and demand, like everything else."

Binnie never knows whether or not to believe his more extravagant assertions. Although it seems to her entirely possible that what he says may be the truth, there is a mischievousness in Edmund that she distrusts. She knows he likes to tease her.

Binnie's Dilemma

"Don't you ever feel detached—cut off—guilty, because you're not more involved with the community, with the real problems?" Binnie asks Vera.

"You mean urban ghettos, juvenile delinquency, draft counselling, political demonstrations, yes? Of course I feel something, but guilty is not the right word, because I know that I, in my own person, cannot possibly take care of all these things. I can only tell myself that what I must do is what I am trained to do, and do it as well as I can. People benefit. They may not be the people whose needs are in the limelight right now, but maybe just because they are not in the limelight they must not be slighted, either! In Germany, it was the same; people suffered. If I believe in the importance of the individual, and I do, then I must believe in the importance of all individuals—even the middle class, yes?"

But Binnie is not satisfied, although she sees and appreciates Vera's point of view. "Vera—how thoughtless I am. For her—how much can you live through in one lifetime—to have lived through Hitler and the concentration camp—not just read about it—to have lost everyone, everything—to have started over, still believing in the importance of the individual—" She doesn't say any of this. But even her casework seems far from the real problems, the festering boils, the suppurating wounds of society. "When it comes right down to it, I'm a frustrated leper-licker. Who would benefit, if I read (at this late date, as I've never been able to bring myself to do) *The Diary of Anne Frank?* And if I quit the hospital, who will benefit? A few people in the slums will get what a few people in the hospital now get, whatever that's worth. I'll get less money, of course, but is that a valid reason either for or against doing it?"

Has Hobart Changed?

When the New Dance Group came to Kiel Auditorium, Hobart asked Binnie if she would like to go with him. Louise was still housebound—that is, she was not only allowed, but encouraged to walk by her doctors, but she had not yet been fitted with her permanent prosthetic appliance. ("Those people down in the shop have a jargon too, you know," Hobart says apologetically. "You should see them—they visibly wince when Louise rolls up, talking about her artificial leg.") Although she gets around very well in the house, she refuses to appear in public.

"Papa Doc's as imperturbable as ever, isn't he," Sarah remarked to Binnie on one of her morning calls at the hospital with Robin in the stroller, giving Hobart the half-admiring nickname bestowed by the irreverent interns (but out of his hearing).

Binnie shook her head. "I'm not so sure it isn't wearing thin. This is all pretty rough on him too, you know." The two of them watched him striding down the hall, his mane of theatrically white hair, which he wears a little longer now, the flying tails of his white coat, suddenly aware of the contrapuntal rhythms of his rapid footsteps and the very faint click of the stethoscope against the heavy silver belt buckle Louise had made for him before the accident, when they came back from Mexico.

"He's still Papa Doc."

Binnie said nothing. When they stopped at her apartment building after the dance program, she had asked him if he'd like to come up for a drink but she was surprised when he accepted. He stayed late, absentmindedly letting her refill his glass several times; his hand brushed her thigh; when he rose to say goodnight she was the first to pull away. "Binnie, dear—"

He glanced hastily at her eyes, wound his scarf around his neck, and turned to go down the stairs. At the foot, he looked up and waved briefly; she was still standing there, watching.

When they encountered each other at the hospital, he made no reference to anything that had happened, but the episode left Binnie feeling uneasy.

The Public and the Private

Rather than be drafted to fight in Vietnam, Susie's boyfriend has gone to Canada. "He's not a coward—but he's not a conshie, either," Susie says. "If he burned his draft card, they'd just put him in jail. What would it prove? I guess some kids have to do it, to make a statement, but not everyone. Why should he have to go to jail, get locked up with all the junkies and perverts, on account of a bad law? When they change the draft law, and Pa says they most likely will, soon, he'll come back. I don't think he's a coward."

"Not even the medieval Church required martyrdom of everyone," Edmund agrees.

"I know some conshies – it's part of their religion. One of the boys I know, he doesn't believe in any kind of killing. He's a vegetarian too, and he wears canvas shoes and elastic belts – stretch, instead of leather, you know."

Edmund continues musing, "The politics of confrontation – surely it isn't necessary for everyone to take that part – or is it? Is the time past already, so quickly past, when a person can live the way he wants to, be what he is, believe what he believes, without rubbing someone else's nose in it? In one way, the openness of your generation, Susie, is great; I've never liked hypocrisy, or approved of it, or enjoyed it. But there are some things that I don't think are any of society's business. Must I ram them in society's face? As Foucault pointed out, it's a bourgeois idea, that virtue is an affair of state."

"Well you know, Edmund, I don't mind at all if a person likes boys better than girls. It doesn't make any difference to me."

"You dreadful child – that's not what I meant at all."

The Friends

In spite of her extensive experience with patients, Binnie is always taken by surprise by her friend Sarah's shifting attitudes. It seems to her only last week that Sarah, having (as she put it) married herself off at last, was rushing from gynecologist to gynecologist, determined to conceive.

"Let's not kid ourselves. I'm no spring chicken," she told Binnie severely, combing her fingers through her really rather beautiful streaky hair, "and Bob and I've been married almost a year, right? So I ought to be pregnant, right?"

Her conversation was swollen with references to fertility studies, sperm count, fertile periods; she was always taking her temperature and recording it on charts. There were charts and calendars everywhere in her pretty little house. Once she even said to Binnie, "Sometimes I think it's a wonder poor old Bob can even manage to get it up anymore." She laughed. "He must feel like a stud," and Binnie privately agreed.

"Don't tell me not to—I know it seems stupid, with all the labs right here in the hospital—" she said one day at lunchtime, "but did you see this ad? There's a private lab downtown that does pregnancy tests in twenty-four hours. The fastest ours will do is three days."

"That's because the quickies aren't as reliable," Binnie pointed out.

"I know, I know, but Binnie—I think I'm pregnant, really I do, and I don't want to wait three days." She gathered up her gloves and her purse and rushed toward the door. "Don't be surprised if I'm a little late getting back."

A week later her suspicion had been confirmed by the current gynecologist and the hospital lab (Binnie never found out what the quickie test had said), and she began having morning sickness: "Poor Bob! Not only having to get his own breakfast, but having to wake up early and bring me crackers in bed—" She was terribly pleased with herself, napping in the nurses' lounge in the afternoons and, after five or six months of that, she quitting work altogether.

Now, less than a year after Robin's birth, she appears in Binnie's office—a rare occurrence. Usually they see each other either in what Sarah insists on calling The Rose-Covered Cottage (and how does Poor Bob like that? Binnie wonders), or in the presence of Bob and one of Binnie's dates, in a restaurant. She is only slightly dishevelled and distraught, and looks blooming; Robin, bundled and wrapped like an infant Eskimo, is with her in a stroller. Perched on the end of Binnie's desk, Sarah confides, "I'm desperate."

"What's wrong?"

"Binnie, I think I'm going to have another baby."

"But, Sarah, that's wonderful–"

An affronted look. "Are you mad? This one–" she shakes the stroller, causing all the plastic bells, rings, keys, and rattles tied to its various railings to jingle, and Robin to laugh aloud, "This one isn't even a year old yet."

"But Sarah–"

"Do you want me to spend the rest of my life without any respite at all, washing clothes and mopping up messes? Have you ever had to spend hours and hours sitting in the playground, listening to other mothers? All they can talk about is baby food and toilet training."

"But Sarah, you're always saying you'd never want an only child. Think how lucky–this time you didn't even have to try to get pregnant."

"–Lucky–!"

Number Of Shocks

after police pushed her, a woman falls onto a
concrete ramp near the Hilton Hotel
CONTINUITY OF DISTURBANCE
pushing a passerby, still astride his bicycle, into
the pond
AREA AFFECTED
was herded by police
against a wall forced through a window and
doused with Mace

SEVERITY OF THE SEQUENCE

finally three policemen picked her up and tossed her
toward the open door of the wagon. But they almost missed
their mark and the girl hit the back of the vehicle.
The officers
picked her up and threw her again

SHORT-TIME STRESS

When he yelled, "I'm a medic!"
the officer said, "Excuse me,"
and hit him again

LOVE WAVES

sprayed with Mace and clubbed on the head as he stood
in his own front yard, he

MAJOR DISCONTINUITY

pulled his men off the demonstrators,
shouting, "Stop, damn you, stop, for Christ's sake, stop it!"

The End of Life

Helen, helpless in the hospital, can't take on the responsibility of Ethel.

Binnie and Grace tell her, "We won't let you take it on. It's ridiculous – you don't realize how bad it's been. She's gotten a lot worse than you think. And besides – think – what would happen to her if you had another attack?"

That is what finally convinces her. "I can see you're right. Ethel would be terrified. She'd be in a panic. She could never manage."

"Yes, and even if she could, somehow, it wouldn't be fair to her to add that burden to her anxieties. You wouldn't want her always worrying about you," Grace puts in shrewdly.

"And then – not that you're going to have another attack,

Helen dear," Binnie goes on, "but if something did happen, then all this would have to be done in a hurry, finding a suitable place for Ethel and convincing her to go there—in the middle of an emergency, when everyone's upset. Isn't it better to let them go ahead and make plans, look into things now, when everybody's calm? You know the present arrangement can't continue."

Helen knows, and yet she is deeply uneasy. "These doctors just want to get rid of her, sweep her under the rug."

Ethel's Dilemma

Ethel has quarrelled with all her friends. She says they have "all turned very difficult. Don't you think a person ought to take the opportunity to improve, if you point out her faults to her?" she asks Helen earnestly, fingering the clasp of her ancient navy blue handbag. "This one particular person—I happen to know why she is the way she is. It's from holding herself in all the time. She never says a word when she talks to her daughter-in-law; she's afraid to antagonize her, so she takes it all out on her friends. The things she's said to me—you wouldn't believe it, Helen! Terrible! I said to her once, 'I know you don't mean those things you say to me when you lose your temper'—she has a terrible temper—'you don't even know what you're saying.' I told her, 'I don't get offended, because I know you don't really mean the terrible things you say to me,' and she said to me, 'I certainly do know what I'm saying, and I mean every word of it.' Can you imagine! —It isn't who you think it is, Helen. Once after I was talking to her I went to the dentist—he's her dentist too, this person's—so when I came in, he asked me, 'How's So-and-so?' and I just burst out crying. I couldn't help crying, tears were just pouring down my face. He said to me, the dentist did, 'What's the trouble?'"

She sniffs violently, snaps open the handbag, and finds a piece of Kleenex, with which she dabs at her nose. "Even Vera—and I used to think she was such a good friend. But *nosy!* And then she had the gall to suggest I ought to make an appointment over on the psychiatric side. I gave her a piece of my mind, you may be sure. 'I thought you were a friend of mine,' I said to her, 'but now I see what you really are. You always were jealous of Ralph and me.' Helen, she didn't dare to say another word."

Many Hundreds

of human beings dead and
alive Can root around in the Salvation Army's
boxes of tattered and faded old clothes for
NO, NOT ME
beauty in negative things, because there was
dirty newspapers, rags, cardboard
stench of burnt plaster and
sodden bedding
"You terrible man," she shouted after
him, I'll never help you!"
WHY ME?
red tape and a hint
of emasculation
oil-soaked muck and by-now putrid
carcasses of drowned horses
"scrubbed, rubbed, varnished,
stuffed, and updated," more to entice than to
wash away every trace of
tiredness in a swirl of
emollient bubbles, and

feel tingly all over!
(rivers of rubbish rushing headlong
BRINGS DEAD THINGS TO LIFE
eternal themes
BARGAINING FOR A STAY OF EXECUTION
in themselves, and as agents
of objects in motion)
with an equal eye. Behavior
as an event
in the cold, vile remains
of the dawn
I AM READY NOW, AND NOT EVEN AFRAID

What Is Happening?

Tessie reports that Ethel gets out of bed and dresses herself at 6:00 A.M. and rings the neighbor's doorbell to find out what time it is.

"She says she can't see the clock. You were right, Helen, her eyes are bad, it's true, Helen."

"But you're right there in the apartment with her. Why doesn't she wake you, instead of bothering the neighbor?"

"If she sees I'm asleep, she doesn't want to wake me. She says she's afraid I'll be angry. It's getting spooky, Helen. You see why I'm getting scared."

Miracles

Since she has been home, sometimes Louise forgets, and starts hurriedly to her feet, only to fall back sideways into the chair, thrown off balance by the leg that ought to have been there holding her up.

"Damn, it feels as if it's there," she says fiercely to Hobart or Vera as she scrabbles for the stick that she is supposed to use temporarily, hopping, when necessary, with its aid. She props it next to her chair, but somehow when she needs it she can never find it. It has either slipped to the floor or insinuated itself into an unreachable corner.

"Soon you will have a new leg—a leg to stand on. A leg that is better than new," Vera says cheerfully.

Louise says, "Vera, if I didn't like you so much I'd throw you out."

"Seriously, these days they can make miracles. You'll see."

Black Power

"So now Hobart has his token spade," Edmund remarks. "Hurray. The hospital is inching its way up from slavery."

Vera says seriously, "One is better than nothing. And there are other nonwhites on the staff."

"One black man, one racist, one liberal, one—no, at least two Jews—I'm talking about Hobart's division—"

"Why are you so bitter always against Hobart?" Vera asks. "He is your friend. Besides, there are many black nurses—several are supervisors. And dieticians—"

"Why doesn't he get rid of Semple?"

"Semple is a good doctor."

"Semple is a racist. For that matter, so's Trudman."

Binnie, coming in with a manila file folder for Vera, says, "What's the trouble now, Edmund? Doesn't Trudman—isn't he interested in playing with you? That's really what's eating him, Vera. It's not Hobart at all."

Likenesses

Much of Edmund's work as a plastic surgeon involves photographs. His office is full of files of folders labelled "One, Two, Three, Four," "Before," "After," "Stage One," "Completion," "Proposed Reconstruction," "Alternate Proposal." From each series of pictures the eyes search him out, pleading, defiant, incurious, mischievous, despairing, unique.

He shivers a little, involuntarily; shakes his head. He prefers to think of himself as an artist, a sculptor in bone and muscle. "Pygmalion!"

"Have you ever noticed how people come to resemble their photographs?" Edmund asks Louise. "You think I'm kidding. What I mean is, often when you look at a photograph of someone you know, you say something like, 'I never noticed those little frowning lines on her forehead,' or, 'his face isn't anything like as wide as that—it makes the shape of his head look altogether different.' But then the next time you look at *her,* you do notice those little frowning lines, and when you see *him,* you see that the shape of his head is different. It's all a matter of lighting and shadows, they say—the impartiality of the camera, which sees everything (and forgives nothing), instead of focusing on a particular feature, as the eye tends to do. I myself always look at a person's eyes—I once knew a woman who claimed the first thing she noticed about a person was the teeth."

A Portrait

which

(solution

technical/aesthetic

of water which

ready-made images

variable/unresistant

complex/horizontal

plane

defeated

with white mineral oil

brilliant arrested

warped, transformed)

a soft material

too far from the viewer at the door

participatory

strains

blown-up overview

linked, clustered, overlapping, random, extensive, diffused, diffuse

The Outsider

Binnie has decided not to believe Edmund's flat statement that Hobart is anti-Semitic. She does, however, believe it's quite likely Hobart is anti-Edmund. Edmund, who never questions the superiority of his eastern training, Edmund, personally arrogant and often insulting, Edmund, simultaneously a Jew and a homosexual. She also believes Edmund could, and would, turn on her—for example—and tear her to pieces, if he felt like it. And that the story of being a foundling left on the steps of the Hebrew National Orphans' Home is pure fabrication.

"How do you think they knew I was a Jew, baby?" asks Edmund, and he sings, *"Soy huerfanito/ Y no tengo padre ni madre / Soy huerfanito / Y no tengo alguien por casarme..."*

Binnie hums the snatch of the song to herself.

Media

Plexiglass
Cast acrylic
Fiberglass
Wax Over Cloth
Milled Aluminum
Flat Enamel on Rolled Steel
Metal Rods and Cord
Painted Wire Mesh
Electrical Wire
Cast Rubber
Acrylic Lacquer and Steel
Tubular Steel
Polyester Resin
Mixed
Media

Marriage

Before Louise and Hobart were married, Louise had made the mistake of thinking Hobart unconventional, partly because he, like herself, would often work straight through the night on some project, oblivious to the hour, the day, Sunday, holidays, seasons, anniversaries, and revolutions. Now she knows that Hobart is simply unaware of any distinction between days. It took her a long time to realize this, and to realize that although he and she frequently behaved in the same way, it was for reasons as nearly opposite as possible. He is unimaginative, rather than unconventional—although, as she has discovered, the two can appear to be the same, and can result in the same consequences.

In some ways, this explains the continued success of their marriage.

A spokesman for the U.S. State Department was quoted as saying that no Americans had been killed in the earthquake that devastated Bucharest, Rumania, flattening apartment houses, buckling streets, and driving thousands of terrified residents from their homes. As rescue workers struggled to free victims from the rubble, fire broke out in many damaged buildings. Survivors roamed through the wreckage, calling out names of relatives and friends. Hospitals were jammed with the injured and the dying. The Intercontinental Hotel, a favorite of Americans, was one of the few structures to escape intact.

IV

Vera's Friendship

Vera says, "It is a terrible blow to your ego that this should happen to your strong, creative sister." She says, "And more, Helen, to see it going on with your sister, someone of your own family and your own generation, that makes it even more of a threat, no? You can't help wondering, will it happen to you?"

She sits perched forward on the visitors' chair, her keen little light-blue eyes missing nothing, stabbing here and there from the bedclothes to the books piled on the night-stand.

Helen says drily, "We understand each other, Vera, you and I. Of course, it's a threat to all of us who knew Ethel and Ralph, but I'd still be glad to take care of her if I could, possibly do it. Rather than send her away."

"You are speaking like a melodrama. For her to be in a nursing home is not to 'send her away.' Most of the time, as I understand it, she doesn't know any more where she is – is she in the office, in the apartment, in the house where she lived before her husband died – she is confused. In a nursing home, she could be just as contented. Your sister Tess, she protects herself. Take my advice. Do the same. And we will do our best for Ethel."

The Appointment

Last week Ethel had an appointment with the eye doctor for Saturday morning at ten; she arrived on Friday, and was infuriated when the doctor refused to see her.

Grace told Helen about it: "She ran through a complete rehearsal, a day ahead of time."

On the Saturday, she arrived again, this time at 8:00 A.M.

and was angry because the office wasn't open and there was no place for her to sit and wait.

"Where was your mother?" Helen wondered.

"She was right there, but Ethel slipped out without saying a word," Grace explained. "I think she realized dimly that there was something wrong with what she was doing, and was afraid that Mother would try to stop her."

Ethel was given a prescription by the doctor, but when Tess asked for it, to have it filled, she told Tess she couldn't find it.

"First she said she couldn't find it," said Grace. "Then she said he didn't give her anything. And then she said she could only find half of it. She refused to admit she must have torn it in half. Now, as a matter of fact, she denies any knowledge of what could have happened. She says the doctor tore it, and only gave her half. I know you think Mother ought to be able to handle her better, and I agree, she probably should – but you know Mother. *She's* not about to change at this late date. And Aunt Ethel is more and more difficult – she's really becoming sly in her attempts to deceive us."

Helen sighed and was forced to agree. None of them were going to change. They were just going to keep on being themselves, more and more.

The Hospital Party

Everyone on the hospital staff always went to the hospital party. Not only doctors and their spouses, but administrators, nurses, lab technicians, physical and occupational therapists, social workers, secretaries, typists, file clerks, and switchboard operators. Louise wasn't going to go this year, but then Hobart, Vera, and Edmund got together and convinced her that she really ought to make the effort.

She came, wearing a ratty-tatty old skirt with her slip showing, and a torn man's shirt (why?). Hobart, by contrast, looking rather splendid in midnight blue chalk stripes with a florid rose pink tie as wide as your arm, patterned with blossoms.

She spent most of her time sitting down, although Vera told Binnie that she had been very regular about coming to the physical therapy classes to learn how to walk with the new leg. Everyone, of course, tried not to look at it (although it looked so natural—you'd never suspect if you didn't know about it). Louise must have felt flattered at so many eyes gazing with such determination directly into hers. The big question, of course, is whether she will be able to do her sculpture again. What a shame she doesn't do something you can do in a wheelchair, or at least without all that moving around and heavy lifting and shoving. That's what everyone was thinking.

What Is Happening to Binnie?

Ever since the night when he invited her to the dance recital at Kiel Auditorium and tried to kiss her when they returned to her apartment for a drink afterwards, Binnie has felt self-conscious in Hobart's presence.

"How do you even know he meant—what you thought he did, Dumdum?" she asks herself. "Probably he was only being friendly."

She feels uneasy with Louise, too. "Displacement," she tells herself. "You're getting the wronged wives mixed up. It's Corinne you ought to be feeling this way about."

But she feels nothing about Corinne.

Instead, she is plagued by imaginary glimpses of Hobart

dishevelled and unkempt in moments of passion, sweaty and incoherent, as she has never seen him in actuality. Sometimes with Louise and sometimes with herself, he is always in attitudes of lust and abandon as far as possible from the way they actually encounter each other.

"Watch it, girl," she admonishes herself. "You'll be turning into a crazy old maid. Next you'll be telephoning the cops, reporting men following you in the street or looking in the window, accusing innocent people of plotting rape." She is only half joking; she senses a real danger.

She has not seen Rich, even casually, around the hospital for about three weeks, and yesterday one of the secretaries mentioned that he is leaving for a stint in California, a visit to a newly organized medical center out there, at the beginning of the month.

"Somebody told me he's thinking of moving out there for good," the girl remarked.

Binnie, feeling as though all the breath had been knocked out of her, said nothing.

Edmund's Gifts

Edmund asks plaintively, "But why should Louise hate me? I simply adore her. Professional jealousy, do you think? We're both sculptors, after all, only I work with real flesh."

It's true that, for some reason, Louise has taken a grand dislike to Edmund, partly, no doubt, thanks to such statements of his. But it is unreasonable of her.

"And I generally get along so well with the ladies," Edmund laments, "Lady artists in especial."

He has sent her, while she was in the hospital and then during her stormy convalescence at home, a series of thoughtfully chosen gifts:

1. a reproduction of an Egyptian figurine
2. a book of Brassai photographs
3. a tiny Japanese garden in a Mexican water bottle
4. a geode of amethyst quartz, split in half and hinged to close again, the two halves polished to a satiny finish
5. a shell of the common angel-wing (*Barnes costata,* fam. Pholadidae)
6. an antique stereopticon viewer, with six slides of bathing beauties of the 1890s
7. a mounted, dried specimen of edelweiss from the Jungfraujoch, framed in passe-partout
8. a record of Josephine Baker singing in French
9. a *mola* sewed by the Cuna Indians of Panama's San Blas Islands
10. a Manhattan telephone directory for the year 1966–67, and
11. a fifth of Napoleon brandy.

Louise says, "Oh my God, I wish he'd stop. Of course I like the things he sends, but I just wish he wouldn't. Why can't I stand that man? It must have something to do with chemistry."

The Strongest Shocks

in twelve years

wrecked two houses knocked
out electric power broke gas &
water mains

still digging out victims
of an earlier
twenty-foot brick wall fell to the
street, damaging

Americum, a man-made isotope
and looting through broken windows
jolted four feet off its
foundations
while half of U.S. adults find
their lives "dull" or "routine"
White, Negro, or Other
with an atomic half-life of 458 years
bodies from the rubble. A steady
rain fell, and
"Mother Nature does not exist," a professor
charged. Increasing the average
concentration of carbon dioxide, reducing
the transparency of the unclouded sky, and
"A number of people are not telling the truth."
Pressure from the lava
expressed discontent. Fifty percent were
apathetic, and eleven percent of those actually wanted
to die

An Evening at Home

When Binnie gets back to her apartment with the groceries, she finds Sue waiting for her. She is wearing pin-striped bell-bottom trousers, an enormous blood-colored plastic ring, and a pince-nez on a gold metal chain. A lank curtain of hair swings in front of her eyes.

"Binnie, say I can stay with you; I just can't go home and face Mother."

"Sure you can." They go into the apartment together, switching on lights; Binnie puts her brown paper bag on the kitchen table. Susie collapses into Binnie's easy chair, fitting a cigarette into her long holder; she has kicked off her shoes; Binnie can see that the bottoms of her feet are dirty.

Sue says, "I think I must be coming down with the flu."

Glancing sharply at her, Binnie sees that her face is suddenly small and yellow, she is sweating, her hair clings damply to her forehead. Clutching her abdomen, Sue lunges toward the bathroom. From behind the not quite closed door come the sounds of retching and gasping, followed by silence, running water, and the toilet being flushed.

"Are you all right?"

"Better now."

On the arm of the chair, smoke writhes from the not quite stubbed-out cigarette. Binnie puts it out. More sounds from the bathroom. After nearly an hour, Sue emerges.

"Come on, you'd better get to bed." Binnie has arranged her own bed for Sue, even putting out a pair of her own clean pajamas. "I'll sleep on the couch this time. Don't be silly! Get to bed." Binnie pulls down the window shades, moves around the room like a nurse. Now her feelings toward Sue are all benign; she is purged of her initial annoyance, the resentment she had felt at her first sight of Sue outside the apartment door, resentment at the mere presence of an intruder, at the notion of having to spend an evening entangled in the strands of Sue's life, at the prospect of having to stay up late while Sue talked—and it's my long day at the hospital tomorrow—with the result that she feels she must have welcomed her cousin with a bad grace, appearing as reluctant as she really did feel. She gathers up Sue's soiled clothes and removes them to the bathroom, gets out rags, a mop, the pail. Cleaning up doesn't disgust her. It seems to her that this is, after all, what Susie came to her apartment to do; as if her vomiting has finally set a kind of seal on the friendship.

A weak voice calls from the further room, "Binnie, if I call you during the night–if I don't feel good–not that I think I will–you'll hear me?"

"Sure I will."

But Binnie wonders, Am I really ready to be a mother to Susie? What about her own mother? Why doesn't she want to face Grace?

> Unlike the Richter scale, the Mercalli scale measures intensity of an earthquake at the particular point where the measurement is taken. Thus, while on the Richter scale the measurement is the same wherever it is measured, the Mercalli varies, depending on the distance from the epicenter of the earthquake.

Happy Families

With apparent irrelevance, Sarah says to Binnie, "You know, my sister Betsy has seven children now."

Binnie has known this for a long time. Before Sarah's marriage she used to accompany Sarah on treadmill tours of the toy departments at Christmas time; she admired snapshots of Betsy, slender and sun-stippled, surrounded by girls and boys, the latest infant swaddled on her knee.

"I used to think I'd like to have five, when I was in high school," she replies.

"Yes, but for Betsy–I mean, a degree in philosophy, a junior Phi Bete–even Phil, that's her husband, I think he's beginning to realize there's something fishy."

"Fishy?"

"Something wrong. What's Betsy afraid of? It's as if something threatens her if she ever gets out from behind her barricade of diapers and nursing bottles. Those babies are protecting her from something." And then, "Don't get me wrong. I love every one of them—she does too—every runny nose and scabby knee. No, really, Binnie, I do; they are sweet. But I don't like what's happening to my sister. She's turning into a cow—a cabbage—a pudding."

Binnie says, "And here I was consoling myself by thinking the world couldn't be in such desperate shape if a professor of ecology and a lady philosopher were willing to bring that many children into it."

In fact, she had both envied and admired Betsy. Maybe that's why I want babies of my own, she thinks, to protect me and release me from responsibility, not the other way round. A license to hide out in the nursery. No need to worry about expectations and demands on me as an individual. Aloud, she muses, "Restful—being a cow, maybe—"

"—oh, Binnie."

The Generation Gap / 3

One of Ethel's sons has come to "do something" about his mother. Helen hasn't seen him for several years, and when he accompanies Binnie on a visit to her in the hospital, she can tell from his face that he finds her greatly changed. For her part, she sees he has grown stout, he is balding, he wears bifocals.

"None of us is getting any younger," she reminds him tartly. "If I weren't stuck in here, I could take care of your mother myself, but between them they've talked me out of it. And your Aunt Tess can barely take care of herself."

It seems to Helen that he is preoccupied mainly with the question of how to get access to Ethel's money.

"We simply can't take the risk of finding ourselves unable to draw money—on her behalf, of course—from her funds at some future date. Why, she can't even write a check any more. This morning I had to tell her exactly what to write, and where to write it. Can you imagine, if some unscrupulous—"

Binnie interrupts, "You'd better watch out, though. You know how paranoid all these old people are. When you start talking about getting control of her bank accounts, she'll think you're stealing from her."

Helen is fretful. "If only I could get out of here and on my feet again, I'm sure I could handle it."

But Binnie says firmly, "Don't make me go through all *that* again. Henry's right, Helen, and you know it. For her own sake Ethel must be moved to a place where she'll be supervised twenty-four hours a day. How would you feel if she were hit on the head one of these nights when she decides to wander around in the street—or if she were picked up by the cops and taken to the state hospital? That's where they'd take her, you know."

The Three Sisters

Once there were three sisters, Helen, Ethel, and Tessie. Helen couldn't wait to get away from home. After she graduated from high school, she learned how to type and take dictation, and went and got a job in New York City.

Ethel met a young medical student and they got married, and then she decided to study medicine herself. Both of them were on the hospital staff. Ralph was Chief of Internal Medicine, known as a brilliant diagnostician and highly respected, even outside St. Louis. Ethel had four sons, and specialized in pediatrics.

Tessie, the youngest, didn't even want to finish high school. In her next-to-last year she got engaged to Leon, who was in his last year of college and about to go into his father's business. The next year they got married, and the year after that their daughter Grace was born.

The Cousins

What about the two cousins, Grace and Binnie? Grace quit college and married Walter six months before he was drafted to fight in World War II. Nine months after the wedding, Susie was born at a base hospital, and five years later Grace and Walter were divorced.

"Oh, you young people," sighed Tess, Grace's mother, herself widowed at an early age. "I just can't understand you. Why—why? Just when Walter was doing so nicely, too . . ."

"Have you thought of the baby?" asked Grace's worried Aunt Ethel, preoccupied with her own family and her professional duties at the hospital.

Grace said nothing, and by the time Susie was in junior high, she found it hard to remember what Walter looked like, although Sue visited him sometimes. She continued to wear her wedding ring (although she sometimes wondered why) and went back to school to get her degree, holding down a full-time job at the same time, since she refused to take alimony.

Binnie, the other cousin, is not married. She has accumulated various degrees in the social sciences in universities of reputable standing, and came to St. Louis to the hospital where her Uncle Ralph headed the Division of Internal Medicine and her Aunt Ethel was on the staff, almost by accident. She has an excellent reputation in her field, and could have a job anywhere.

"Binnie, she's so attractive, she's so bright, she knows

so many interesting men—how come she isn't married?" Tess asks her daughter Grace, but she does not dare ask Binnie.

Looking back, Binnie herself can't put her finger on any one decision, any single choice that led her to where she is now, sitting behind her desk with its neat blotter and crowded calendar, a hand-thrown stoneware pitcher holding a few jonquils standing on top of the filing cabinet.

The two cousins, while not exactly friends, are half-aware of sharing an uneasy alliance. Each one, seeing the other, thinks, "That might have been I."

The Three Old Ladies

Many years later, after the old ladies went, it seemed to their niece Binnie that theirs had been a remarkable survival, that they had all three lived remarkable and even significant lives, although she would have found it difficult to say why, or even how. Three such different, distinct personalities, three such dogged individuals, don't disappear without a trace! But they are gone now; even their tortoiseshell toilet sets with the gold initials have been given to the Goodwill, and the old yellowed photographs with their outlandish clothes and frozen postures don't resemble anyone. The old letters and bills have made nests for mice or kindled fires in ornamental fireplaces; somewhere, perhaps, a trace of their handwriting lingers in the drawer of an old desk, overlooked by daughters-in-law or grandchildren.

Scientists have found that the seismic waves generated by an earthquake have a wide range of period. Some may last less than a tenth of a second, while some may continue indefinitely. Those that last longest correspond to the deformation of the ground around the fault, while the shortest actually come within the low audible range. Waves with periods of about one hour have a frequency that coincides with the resonance frequency of the earth, and can cause the earth itself to ring like a giant bell.

The Problem

This morning when Helen phoned Ethel's son Henry he took a different tone. "I've a man waiting to see me; I can't talk very long."

He had seen his mother again last night. She was perfectly rational, and just like her old self. She denied everything and told him, "You believe all the lies they tell you about me."

"But, Henry–!" Helen protested.

"Oh, I know, you're the ones I believe, Aunt Helen, I know you and Grace and Binnie aren't making up these stories. But she sounded so sensible, and she promised not to do anything to worry anybody, like going out at night. Really, Aunt Helen, she's perfectly aware of what the problem is."

The Portrait

Louise, squinting up under tawny eyebrows from the padded, buttressed redoubt of her armchair, looks critically at Hobart where he sits frowning slightly over *The New Statesman,* which they receive by subscription, a gift from the secretaries at the hospital.

"What does he see, when he looks at himself?" she thinks.

1. A successful physician in middle-age.
2. A graying but still handsome lover.
3. A repository of countless secrets.
4. A thoughtful citizen.
5. A conscientious householder.
6. A pillar of society.
7. A distinguished member of the professional community.
8. A mature male, somewhat fleshy, virile, height six feet two inches, 187 pounds, eyes 20/20,

Bronzed,

White-maned,

Clear-eyed,

Firm-lipped,

Solid,

Upright,

Trustworthy,

Sincere,

Reliable? Hands (can see, looking down); thickening waist. Feels the stubble on his jaw (now white)? Surrounded by the objects, chairs, tables, sofas, curtains, carpets, beds, dressers, bookcases, boxes, pictures all created by their marriage.

She wants to *be* Hobart. To feel to see to hear smell breathe itch to be hungry thirsty tired horny, being Hobart.

But only as a beginning. To experience as another. Outside the prison of self. The beloved prison. To break out, beyond–not in order to abandon self, her self, but to share–even for an instant–the experience of the Other–what an impossibility!

An absurdity!

Hunched in her chair, Louise thinks, "His crippled wife."

Louise Is Working

Louise has started working again. Nobody knows what she is doing. She has not been out in the old studio in the garage since the accident; the metal sheets, the wire, and the pipes lie out there, rusting and corroding. The tools, put away with meticulous care by Hobart while she was in the hospital, are in their locked compartments, the power has been turned off, and the heavy door is padlocked.

Now Louise has taken over the small room off the upstairs hall. She asked Hobart to move in a table and a straight chair from the garage studio, as well as the high-intensity lamp, which he had brought into the house to protect from the damp, and every morning when he leaves for the hospital she goes in there and closes the door.

"I phoned you the other day; I let it ring at least twenty times! I knew you were there in the house somewhere and I just didn't like to hang up," Vera scolds her. "I was worried that something had happened to you."

"I'm working," Louise replies briefly. "I disconnect the upstairs phone so it doesn't ring, and when I'm up there I can't hear the ringing in the kitchen."

Not even the cats are allowed into the room where she works.

Blue Stockings

"But, Vera, you're in no position to talk; you've had children."

"Yes, I have had children."

It is of no importance, for the moment, that Vera's children—as Binnie did not happen to know, for if she had she would never have introduced such a painful subject—are a series of calamities, one a lifetime resident of a Sheltered Home, one a dedicated member of a secret Israeli terrorist group, the third dead twenty years.

"Even Margaret Fuller, the American bluestocking par excellence, desperately wanted to have a child. She said, 'The woman in me so craves this experience it seems the want of it may paralyze me . . .'"

Vera gives Binnie a kindly look. "Yes, you are right. There is something in every woman, I think, a voice that says to her, 'This is your birthright. Never to hold your own child in your arms is to be cheated of your birthright, what you were born for.' But all the same, I do not believe this voice is always right."

"In two years I'll be thirty-five. Sometimes I think – if I'm not married by then – I'll have a baby anyway. I hate unmarried, childless women in their forties, getting shriller – I don't want to be one."

Vera says, "Don't be one, then! But you must not think having a child is going to change that."

Edmund and Louise

Edmund has spent a lot of time pondering Louise's condition, in a vain attempt to sympathize with Louise, to feel himself into her sense of herself. The attempt is in vain, because consciously, at any rate, Louise almost never thinks about her missing leg any more. Her energies, once they have been deflected from raging at the fact of the accident, have all been directed toward finding a new and feasible way of working. She was irritated by having to go to classes at the hospital to learn to use what the therapists insisted on calling her prosthesis, chiefly because the appointments broke into her working time. She sometimes, even now, curses the limb itself, but almost absentminded-ly, the way you might swear at a dog or a child that gets it-self stepped on because it didn't get out of the way in time. Mostly, these days she is too busy to pay any attention to it at all.

Especially Resilient

pastry displays, clothing, graffiti,
advertisements, people, even debris
foam plastic, soft to the touch
the straps, and then
plunge into and grope around in
a sea of people, learning how to put on
wood covered with plastic
backwards, sickeningly, through the
wet, filthy air and slammed down
wearing two corsets and a
waist belt to which straps are hooked.
Going up
unconscious all night across a heap
of drifting wreckage, his face and
arms badly torn and nearly
blinded in one eye by sand and lime
Holding onto parallel bars,
aluminum crutches and
finally, two canes
Going down
Then pushing her body backward
she propelled herself
standardized, specialized, frag-
mented, and beautifully packaged
BUT WHAT IF

she were caught.

in a fire, crackling and splitting, and

without her leg?

The air was filled with flying boards & broken glass,
"as much Nature for me as the countryside was for Cezanne."

A Sly Old Woman

The doctor has told Helen that she can leave the hospital next week. "But I strongly recommend that you go into a nursing home for a week or two," he says. "If you go home you'll start doing too much, and before you know it I'll have you back here again."

"I live with my sister – my sister," she protests. "I won't have to do anything; we're both at home."

Especially now that she has agreed that Ethel must move to a nursing home, the prospect of finding *herself* there among the incontinent old women, their bosoms spotted with egg yolk (they dab at it with trembling, old, spotted hands), who sit at the window, waiting – always hungry – is impossible, unthinkable. And the old men who need to be reminded to do up their zippers, with stained trousers and speckled shirtfronts, ropy arms hanging out of their shirtsleeves, feet shuffling in house slippers – they sit hunched over the TV, thumbing through the papers, turning over the day's mail, in the next room somebody fitfully, weakly crying *oh, oh, somebody help me – somebody please help me –*

Helen looks the doctor straight in the eye and says briskly, "I promise you, Doctor, I won't lift a finger at home."

But he shakes his head. "Do me a personal favor. Only one week in a nursing home. I'd keep you here, if beds weren't so tight. You can afford it – be sensible. One week."

She looks away. "Very well then, if you think it's really essential."

But she has no intention of going.

When she tries to examine her own motives in refusing to go, she finds nothing rational; only a cold, unshakable voice that stubbornly repeats, "Not me. Not yet. I'm not ready! Not me."

She recognizes the voice as the expression of all her most secret fears; she hears in it Mom-mom's, her mother's, voice, begging breathily, "Don't send me away—to die—not yet—don't send me," and even farther back, echoing out of her long-ago childhood, her grandmother's voice, "That's where they send you to die, I know all about it, I won't go, I won't go," while Mom-mom tried to reassure her, "Nobody's going to die, you'll see, it's easier to take care of you there, that's all . . ." But she died.

And she hears Ethel's voice; it turns, dreadfully, into her own, insisting against all reason (and doesn't reason tell her that it will be only for a week, a week of cranked-up beds and meals on trays?), "Not yet! Not me! I'm not ready to go there yet."

On the day she leaves the hospital, walking out quite steadily without Tessie's arm, although she has permitted Binnie to carry her suitcase, Helen says to herself, "You're turning into a sly old woman. In spite of all the doctor said, here you are, doing what you intended to do all along."

But instead of feeling ashamed, she is aware of a flicker of pride. Unlike her grandmother, unlike Mom-mom, unlike Ethel, she is still able to make her own choices. The pride she feels is in that voice inside her, calm, obstinate, invincible, still repeating, "Not me. Not yet. I accept the responsibility for my choices."

Helen and Sue

How beautiful the world was – even twenty years ago when Helen was still living in New York, still in the first flush of the UN Charter, rebuilding Europe, the lights going on again all over the world – even on West Fourth Street, on Charles Street, the very pavements glittered, doors opening up everywhere, and in the heady air, particles of soot dancing and shimmering like angels.

Helen has just heard, through Tess, that Tessie's granddaughter Sue has gone off to New York. Nobody knows where she is or what she is doing.

"Poor Sue," Helen thinks. "To have missed those times, those wonderful times in the forties – when everything was still possible. How she would have loved it! She could have stayed with me –" and then she has to laugh at herself. "Lucky Sue, she's there now in the sixties – and who knows what the seventies will bring? The sidewalks are sparkling for her, smog and all. Twenty years old, in New York for the first time – that's all that counts, all the rest is just statistics and bad news in the papers."

Because man-made structures are particularly susceptible to earthquake damage, due to the fact that seismic waves have frequencies that coincide with the resonant frequencies of such structures, and because major earthquake motion is usually in the horizontal plane rather than in the vertical, structural engineers, builders, architects, and designers in earthquake-prone regions must take special precautions to counteract these two forces.

Wolf's Death

Toward the end, just before the outbreak of war in Europe, it seemed to Helen that she spent most of her time trying to keep Wolf from being beaten up by taxi drivers (all of whom, he believed, were conspiring to cheat and humiliate him) or jailed by the police. After being robbed and left unconscious in an alley by a group of youths he had picked up at Duffy's Bar, he suffered from excruciating headaches which made it more and more impossible for him to sleep. The good days were few and far between. She was hardly surprised by the final telephone call summoning her to St. Vincent's Hospital, where he had been taken in the police ambulance.

When she got there, hot, perspiring, out of breath (for it was July, the first July of the war), through some mix-up she was not allowed to see him in the emergency room. By the time the misunderstanding had been straightened out, Wolf was dead.

Area Of Major Disturbance

3,000 sq. mi., approx. 100 mi. from Cairo, Ill. to
Memphis, Tenn., and approx. 50 mi. east-west
altered stress pattern
She bent over her
husband as he lay bleeding from the wound near
his right ear and another in his shoulder, whispering to him
and trying to console
three distinct shocks felt
without instruments in Detroit (600 mi.) and Boston (1100
mi.). Total area of
1,000,000 sq. mi., half the continental United States, was so

disturbed that

ONE OF THE NATURAL HAZARDS

with which man must live, but

with impairment of the blood supply to that part of the brain
that governs the eye track, the level of
consciousness and . . .

the speech centers

after a mass

of broken tissue emerged the head was born, to everyone's
horror, and the deformed fetus began to cry

A SEVERE JOLT

was the time-tested formula of being shocked and
disgusted by
the details, while spreading them all over

exceeding the severity

of the San Francisco quake of 1906 and Alaska in 1964
Theoretical calculations suggest velocities approached 90 mph
and the thickness of the turbidity current reached 900 ft.

THE FAULT ZONE

"I told my mother about it and she thought it was
immoral."

In Edmund's Apartment

Nobody knows, except Edmund and Susie themselves, exactly what happened in Edmund's apartment before Susie took off for New York. Binnie knew as much as anyone, because Sue spent the afternoon, beforehand, with her. She has gone over it in her mind dozens of times, but cannot find in it any clues that might lead to an explanation of Sue's behavior afterward.

"She seemed excited – like any girl looking forward to a date – but cool, you know."

Sarah, tasting her coffee, says, "After all, she's experienced, not an ingenue," by which she means, not a virgin.

Binnie agrees, "I'm sure she's gone to bed with her boyfriend–she says she does; most of the kids do, I guess. I don't think it's that."

Sarah says, "What about him? Edmund–he must know she's gone off. Doesn't he say anything?"

"He knows she went, of course; my aunts told him so; I was there. But he just raised his eyebrows in that theatrical way he has, and gazed at us with those melting eyes. I think he said, 'pretty little black-eyed Susie, I'll miss her,' and went on humming."

"You never did like Edmund," says Sarah.

"I don't trust him. As a person, I mean, not as a doctor. I think he's a very good surgeon. But under that phony sympathetic manner of his, I think he really loathes women, and if I ever turned my back on him I'd actually expect to get a knife in it."

"It's funny, because I always thought he liked you," says Sarah.

Binnie is impatient. "I know. I think he thinks so, too. And I enjoy talking to him; he's so intelligent, and so damned knowledgeable, about things besides medicine, I mean. But deep down he hates me–and if he could do me dirt without soiling his hands (you see, that comes into it too), he wouldn't hesitate. And I think that goes for you, too, and for Susie, too–and with her he somehow got his chance. I just hope he didn't really hurt her."

"Don't worry; she's young, and they're tough. Really tough, in the good sense," Sarah says comfortably.

Permanence and Change

At the hospital, everything goes on very much as usual. The wide pale green corridors are full of the subdued rustle, creak, shuffle, whisper, and hum of starched uniforms, rubber-soled shoes, wheelchairs and stretchers rolling along, patients in bathrobes and slippers, visitors talking in voices self-consciously muffled, nurses and aides with charts and thermometers, technicians, residents, and students preoccupied and hurrying. Fathers, sisters, daughters, anxious relatives stand before the banks of elevators, noticeably foreign among the natives of the place.

Binnie, hurrying along (she has to get back to her office for an appointment), thinks that actually it's for the benefit of those intruders that the whole complex machine hums. The building was built for them. And at any moment, one of "us" can turn into one of "them" – Ralph, and then Helen, for so many years habitués of the green corridors – how strange it had felt, going to visit them as patients, they who were so much more at home here as one of the cogs, however small, that keeps the whole vast machine going.

A First Date

Binnie is going to a concert with Derek Trudman.

"I don't remember how to behave on a first date," she tells Helen. "What do I say? 'How did you ever come to be called Derek?' I mean – that name is so damned British! It's all I can think of. He'll think, what did I expect, that he'd be called Sambo?"

Item: Degrees from U. of P. and Columbia
Item: Plays the cello

Item:Tall and handsome
Item:Black

Did Tessie Ever Grow Up?

Did Tessie ever grow up? Tessie did not grow up for many years, not until long after her only daughter, Grace, was grown and gone, and Grace's daughter, Sue, had left in her turn. Even in widow's weeds Tess had continued to play at her life, although she wept as much as any other widow, with puffed and reddened eyes and an empty bed. Moving back into the roomy old apartment with her two older sisters, she felt at home, but she had felt that way in her own comfortable home, bringing up Grace according to the recommendations of the pediatricians of the day and steaming vegetables in a patented waterless cooker to conserve their vitamins.

If Leon had not died, then, would she have been a different person? Impossible to determine. You might say it was his indulgence of her as child-bride that led her to view herself indulgently. She placated herself with little gifts, rewarded herself with chocolates, soothed her loneliness with ice-cream sodas, éclairs, blueberry cheesecake, and whipped cream.

The Miracle

Vera stops Hobart in the corridor at the hospital to say, "How is Louise these days; how is she progressing?"

"She's fine, just fine," he replies heartily, automatically glancing at his watch.

"I promised you a miracle; I said she would go back to

working again!" cries Vera, laying her plump, capable little hand briefly on the starched sleeve of his white coat.

"Yes, yes, she's fine," replies Hobart, and he strides away down the corridor, already late for a meeting.

No News From Sue

And still nobody has heard from Susie; nobody knows where she is living or what she is doing.

Her grandmother, Tess, worries, clutches her bosom in one of those classic gestures that Helen is always astonished to encounter in real life, and makes long-distance telephone calls to her friends in all five boroughs of New York. None of them, to nobody's surprise, has heard from Susie.

Grace, Sue's mother, shrugs her shoulders in public and prays, passionately, in private, to the God whose existence she doesn't believe in.

Helen says, "Hang on, Grace. If she lives through it, she'll be all the better for it," but she herself wonders, privately, and worries. If she doesn't live through it? She thinks, "Sue was a sweet child, staying with us when she was small – Miss Muffet – eating rice and milk for her supper, just as Grace did when she came to stay when she was small, and I'd put some raisins in the rice for a surprise . . . I'd move one of the chairs from the dining room in next to the sofa to keep her from falling off in the night – she wasn't used to sleeping in a bed without a railing." And then she thinks, "Damn it, Sue, you could at least send a card, or call – making us all worry like this – "

A man in California claims that he can predict earthquakes by means of calculations based on the phases of the moon and maps of weak places in the earth's crust. Using the concept that the gravitational force of lunar tides triggers the release of accumulated strain on the continental plates, he says he can predict where and when shifts in land mass will occur.

The Visit

The prospect of visiting Ethel has filled Helen with enormous apprehension for three days. A sound sleeper all her life, she wakens at two in the morning, before first light, and can't fall asleep again, every nerve humming with fear.

"I'm a terrible coward, Binnie," she confesses. "I think, if I'd been able to go right away, it wouldn't have been so bad, but having been laid up myself for such a long time, and having to put it off—I'm afraid to see what Tessie and I have done to Ethel."

"Nonsense," scolds Binnie. "You and Tessie haven't done anything to Ethel except protect her. She has deteriorated noticeably—you'll see. But that's why she's there, that's why she couldn't be left alone in the apartment. Because this deterioration was inevitably bound to occur."

But Helen sighs, and shakes her head. She is not comforted.

No News from Sue

And still nobody has heard from Susie, nobody knows where she is living or what she is doing.

V

What Is It Like?

Some may be spurious, and due to errors in calculations of
depths and velocities resulting from dipping layers,
misinterpretations, and
incorrect assumptions about the structure
of groups of people, terrified
setting off on aimless expeditions,
threatened by fire or col-
lapsing walls and turning back
energy emanating from out of the
INARTICULATE NAIVETE
This visual measurement of the movement may not be
complete, plotted as dashed lines
theoretical curves taken from
signals not receivable by
standard equipment
in phase with certain vibrations,
loveless and solitary, no
matter what
neither above nor below
(Ah, c'mon man, it's a put-on)
emptiness of the persona
touched the nerve of
failure to respond to
consider the effects of unknown or
poorly known
TRANSCURRENT FAULTINGS
have their origins in
love scenes filmed in a transparent
plastic bed
gory car wrecks, race riots, the electric chair,
mourning Jackie
Kennedy,

publicity photos of Liz Taylor and Marilyn Monroe
THE "MOST WANTED"
cities connected by an earthquake track
grow fat on corpses trapped in
the debris. The
velocities V of longitudinal and $\surd$ *of transverse*
waves in km/sec are about $V=6+/-\surd=3\text{-}1/2+/-$ *in the*
pervasive fatalism and fright
unpredictable distortions, feelings of strangeness, a sense of
beauty in common objects, sometimes fear
and panic and even psychosis.

The First Shock

At the time of the first shock, Tessie was standing in front of a display of toothbrushes in Katz's Drugstore at the corner of Seventh and Locust. The image that flashed through her mind, from far back in childhood, was standing on a wooden railway bridge while a train passed over it. The same rumble and clatter, the thrilling of the soles of her feet, the throbbing of the floor beneath them. More puzzled than frightened, she looked into the face of the woman standing next to her and found it gray with alarm, the mouth beginning to open, the eyes fixed on shelves where bottles and jars, boxes and canisters had begun to dance and trot.

A moment later, when the contents of the shelves had begun to rain down onto the floor, she found herself standing outside in the street in the center of a small group of people all looking skyward, where there was nothing to be seen. The sound had stopped, and there was nothing to be felt. If it had not been for the fact that they were all standing there in attitudes of apprehension and alarm she would have thought nothing had happened. The sidewalks and façades of the buildings were all intact, and, in fact, all that could be seen anywhere were small groups of people all talking and gesticulating.

Somewhat sheepishly, she and the others returned to the drugstore, where she was, perversely, reassured to see the debris of displays and merchandise, shattered glass and toppling masonry – it proved that something out of the way had actually taken place.

Consider Lisbon, for Example

for at that time
the great truths of religion were
ridiculed, the people blasphemed
in the streets, and made lewd pictures
illustrating all the abominations
of the public stews
homosexuality
craze for amusement
debauchery, and
OPTIMISM ATTACKED
although Hodgson has solved a Queen Charlotte Island
shock of
August 12, 1949, and a British Columbia shock of June 23,
1946. I myself have solved an earthquake off the coast of
California
O CIEL, SECOUREZ-MOI!
although prolongation
beyond the theoretical limit is a phenomenon nearly always
observed.

The Earthquake

The decorous hospital corridors were suddenly awash with rumor.

"Earthquake – two tremors – Richter scale – seismograph on the radio! Damage downtown – bricks – falling – the Arch is swaying –"

Patients calling for a nurse pressed their buzzers, and at the nursing stations all the lights flashed on at once. But the nurses were too busy to answer the calls. They were all talking to each other about it: "I thought – it must be me, looked up and there's the cabinet going up and down on the wall! Oh, brother, that must have been a bad one – wonder if it's over, or – the TV – must be more to come – they said – always aftershocks – good grief, I started on my rosary –"

"Nurse, nurse! What happened, nurse?"

"What's happening, nurse?"

"Nurse, I need a nurse!"

According to the National Earthquake Information Center, earthquakes in the past have killed more than 1,500 people in the United States. There are no reliable figures on the number of shocks and the duration of each shock required to destroy these lives. Nor are there figures on the duration of the shocks required to destroy Antioch (A.D. 526), Lisbon (1755), or Tokyo and Yokohama (1923), killing 250,000; 60,000; and 200,000 people, respectively.

Those who have experienced tremors and shocks, of whatever magnitude, report that while the convulsions of the earth are in progress, it is impossible to estimate the passage of time, that one second can seem as long an an hour, and six seconds can take on the aspect of eternity.

What To Do

Dean Richard H. Jahns of the Stanford University School of Earth Sciences reports that the Japanese advise people to count to 30 before doing anything during an earthquake.

"When the earth first begins to tremble, it is best for residents to stay inside a one-family house, generally under an archway. The natural impulse is to run, to flee, to escape, but that's just about the time the house will start collapsing and the person will be struck down by a crashing beam or an onslaught of bricks," Dr. Jahns said.

"After counting to 30, which is what the Japanese do, it might be prudent to go outside to a spot away from trees or power poles."

Helen at Home

Helen was in the kitchen when she felt the first shock, or heard the first rumbling sound. She never could be sure which actually came first. Her first thought was that a plane coming to land at the airport had crashed near the house, then that there had been some sort of explosion in a gas main; at the same time, part of her brain registered something familiar about the sensation. It was like a great quantity of snow sliding off the roof in ski country. All these things were in her mind simultaneously; she was not alarmed. And yet the shaking, transmitted through the soles of her feet, of the kitchen floor, the very foundations of the house seeming to quiver and shift, communicated some degree of anxiety; she ran to the front window.

In the calm suburban street nothing had happened. She saw no one, no smoke or debris, no evidence of calamity.

"As usual," she said to herself, letting the curtain fall back into place. She ran back to the kitchen and turned on the radio there, and it was then that she heard reports of the earthquake.

By that time it was all over. Half an hour later, she noticed that she was trembling and her hands were shaking. She had been reminded that her life, which she had believed herself ready to relinquish last fall on the day she awoke to find herself in the hospital, was still dear to her. Even the featureless suburban street, edged with spindly trees recently planted to replace the towering old silver maples and elms, partook of the timeless and universal. Is there a point at which mere survival becomes moral? When simple endurance becomes Everlasting Life?

What Happened

. . . Officials believe twenty-five persons are missing, some buried in the rubble of the collapsed buildings. Forty-two deaths were reported, none of them heart attack victims. More than one thousand were reported injured.

The shock at 10:01 A.M. yesterday was centered twenty-six miles northwest of downtown, causing damage likely to be in the hundreds of millions of dollars. Hundreds of commercial buildings and factories were damaged, along with uncounted houses, highways, bridges, and public buildings.

Authorities said it might be another day or more before all victims could be reached. Cries of "Help me! Help me!" could be heard from the rubble.

Binnie's Life

Binnie, whose Eastern upbringing had not prepared her for earthquakes—to her they were something that happened in Tokyo or San Francisco, in spite of the fact that three minor tremors had occurred and been reported in the *Post-Dispatch* in the years since she had come to St. Louis—was at the hospital when it began. Afterwards, she found it hard to believe that the whole thing had lasted only six seconds. It seemed to her to stretch out interminably after she realized what was happening.

It was not exactly that her whole life passed before her eyes, as it is said to do for drowning men, but that she was aware of being suffused with regret for not having used her life better, for having let it slip and drift through her fingers, so that when it seemed to her that she might be experiencing its last few seconds, every sensation became intolerably vivid and at the same time poignant, and when the earth had settled into immobility once more, she found herself sitting at her desk holding out two fists clenched in a physical effort to cling to a single instant in time.

Nature of the Source

a rumbling noise that to many people
    sounded like exceptionally heavy traffic
        in an adjacent street
                tied to his cot and burned
            to death; another found hanged by his belt
            after he begged to be moved from his
                cell for fear of being killed, and
            PNEUMATOLOGIA
convulsed with major shocks

miserable sick inmates of the
burning hospital dumped down, ex-
posed & helpless

OR "MATERIA ELECTRICA"

no divine visitations
reaching instantly to the upper
caverns & exploding combustible gases
(however, there is no evidence that there was
such a force in antiquity)

PERPETUAL FIRES RAGING

. . . attacked sexually three more times
for the destroyers of our houses, palaces, and churches, and the cause of death of many and of the flames that devoured, are your own abominable sins!

For reasons no one has as yet fully understood, many of the major earthquakes reported have occurred either in sparsely populated regions of the earth, or so early in the morning that most offices, streets, and public buildings are virtually empty.

(Nevertheless, the threat is almost refreshing to some.)

Edmund Is Angry

Edmund had never intended to stay in St. Louis longer than one year. He came because of Dr. Roeder, the celebrated burn man, whose fame had reached even to the coasts, and now, three years later, he was not at all sure what was keeping him here. The earthquake filled him with indignation. It was an affront, an insult, an outrage; it threatened his very humanity, his manhood, and the secret core of his being.

Standing off from the violence of his own response, he observed it, as he frequently did observe his own emotional responses, with some slight surprise. It occurred to him that the strength of his indignation was in an inverse ratio to the actual damage the earthquake had done him; if he had been injured, or even severely shaken up, instead of merely enduring an unfamiliar and frightening sensation for—what was it—six seconds, then (more than likely) his main response would have been a feeling of relief that things hadn't been worse. As it was, he felt angry that nature—the universe—should have the power to affect him at all. As a sentient, highly rational product of civilization, he should be immune to such blind, haphazard forces. Furthermore, if he had not happened—*happened,* he repeated to himself in italics, quite accidentally to be in St. Louis, Missouri, of all the unlikely places on the map, he would never have been subjected to such an absurdity. How simple it would be if one could only believe that thus a wrathful deity punished sinners! For although he had long since discarded the idea of Sin, he knew himself to be a sinner.

Faults

caused by
            change in dip of
                        criteria for
the relation to the formation pattern
                        strain applied to
"MOTHER NATURE DOES NOT EXIST,"
                        ENVIRONMENT GROUP TOLD
grooving along
    normal
        oblique
            parallel
                pivotal

radial
rotational
stretching
striking
tearing
thrusting
side-slip
strike-slip
trace-slip (topographic expressions)
. . . but the terms are meaningless, if
"The cost is more than the average American is prepared to pay."

Beyond Belief

"All I can say is, it's beyond belief. Those chimneys crashing through the roof and into the basement. They broke some six-by-ten beams like they were kindling," said Mrs. R. M. "I can't reach my husband. Can you get in touch with him and tell him the boys and I are all right?" she asked. "But what I really want to know—and would you please ask him—is, do we have earthquake insurance?"

"The woman upstairs came down screaming," said an apartment dweller. "She said even the bolted-down toilet seat flew off. Then she got in her car and drove away."

A housewife said, "The water cooler broke and about four gallons of water went all over the floor. Lamps toppled, dishes fell, and out front the sidewalk cracked. Windows were rattling like someone was pounding them with a sledgehammer."

"It woke me up and I said, 'Jesus,' and ran toward the kids' room," said a young father. "They were already crying. They looked as if they were riding in a bobbing rowboat. The strange rumbling that accompanies earthquakes had already subsided by the time we grabbed them from their beds and headed out the door. As we drove down the boulevard, heading nowhere, I noticed block after block of stores where windows had been smashed and burglar alarms were ringing. Natural gas hissed from a fissure near the cross street. By now we could hear dozens of sirens in the distance."

A Miracle Could Happen

Tessie claims that since she started taking gifts of food prepared by herself to Ethel, Ethel has gained three pounds. She brings jars of chicken fricassee or lentil soup, bratwurst and sauerkraut, homemade potato salad, squares of crumb cake or gingerbread.

"It's like a picnic! And sometimes she talks very rationally; you wouldn't believe it. You never can tell – a miracle could happen and she could come back home again to live."

She has forgotten that it was largely because of her, because she refused (quite rightly) to keep Ethel at home, that Ethel went to the nursing home in the first place.

Wolf and History

It seems to Helen, who will never write her projected biography, or even a personal memoir of Wolf Tombey (nor will she sort and organize his papers), that the great events of History are inevitably seen by later generations in monolithic terms. The building of the Great Wall of China, the Fall of the Roman Empire, the signing of the Magna Carta, the Industrial Revolution, the assassination of the

Archduke Ferdinand at Sarajevo, the Japanese attack on Pearl Harbor—all of these appear in the history books as if they and their manifold side-effects, always lasting for many years and sometimes for many centuries, were, like the shocks of an earthquake scientifically calibrated on the Richter scale, capable of being not only identified and labeled, but measured with some degree of precision.

"It's not so," Helen thinks with some degree of surprise that she could have been misled so long. Any event, (whether historical or geological), while it's in progress, is experienced only in fragments by each individual experiencing his or her fragment of it. It's only later that the pattern appears, superimposed on the event. The very trembling of the earth, afterward to be noted by its force and duration, the amount of damage caused and number of lives lost, seems at the moment of its occurring to exist outside of time, as if it must continue forever. As if total destruction, even annihilation of the experiencing self, is the only conceivable outcome. And yet History persists in viewing the past as if it were composed of materials quite different from the helter-skelter, chaotic flurry of "givens" and "receiveds" that make up the fragmentary present.

Hard as it is to believe, she knows that in ten or twenty years everyone will have forgotten what it was really like in the sixties. That turbulent, wonderful, terrible decade, which opened with Jack Kennedy and the fairy tale of Camelot, when it seemed, all too briefly, the age of Aquarius was really at hand. The sixties—decade of the children's crusades that "for one brief shining moment" rekindled hopes that had seemed dead, hopes for a world remolded closer to the heart's desire—crusades doomed as those of the medieval children had been doomed. A decade of the Provos in Holland, of hundreds of thousands of peace marchers in England, Europe, and America, of students all over the world afire with idealism and energy. A decade coming to a close now, bloodied by three vicious assasinations, with one of the nastiest, most shameful wars in our history, with the nation turning on its own flower-children, beating and clubbing them, gagging and gassing them and throwing them into prison—it will all be smoothed out and glossed over until a pattern emerges that's been invisible while we were living though it.

"Even Wolf's life," she thinks; "how he would have sneered at the notion of significant form in it. And yet, now enough time has passed so even I can see it as another piece of the pattern of how artists lived in, and were destroyed by, the world between the wars—although at the time we couldn't even know that was the 'period' we were living through, having no way of foreseeing the inevitability of World War II . . ."

Wolf himself, even for Helen, has gradually turned from a living, suffering being whose every painful breath tormented her—his frustrations and rages having left their indelible marks, like bruises, on her body and spirit—into a figure in literary history. Not that she would deny his suffering, but she sees it now as a completed figure, not merely part of the dance of the past, but almost itself a historical event.

Growing Up

"What marriage, nor motherhood, middle-age, and widowhood have been unable to do," Helen thought, "Susie is doing to her grandmother. Not that it'll make any difference to Susie, or make Grace's life any easier, but Tess actually does seem to be growing up at last."

How People Change

"Hobart's changed, hasn't he," Sarah observed. "It's being Division Chief."

Binnie, who still feels oddly self-conscious in Hobart's presence, said, "Changed–how?"

"He never used to be a fanny-pincher, for one thing," said Sarah calmly. "Just watch; even the way he looks at the nurses is different. He never used to see them at all–as if the girls were machines or something. I don't know, but he never looked at them as if they were *girls*. Then for a while it was almost as if he thought they were people. But now it's something else again–like a sultan looking over his harem, or something."

She was sitting in Binnie's patients' chair, touching up her nail polish from a glistening red bottle she had brought with her in her large Italian leather handbag. The baby, sitting at her side in the stroller, looked attentively from one face to the other. Since she had become reconciled to her new pregnancy, Sarah had taken on a new serenity, her complexion had a cool, waxy sheen–"like a cabbage," she said, "and I feel like one, too." She gave up sitting on desks and tended to trundle herself along as she walked, rolling slightly from side to side, although the thickening at her waist was still barely perceptible.

"Male change of life," Binnie said idly.

"No, it isn't, and it's not his wife's accident, either. I've seen it before, it's the Success Syndrome. But I never expected to see it in Hobart. He's not the type."

As usual, Binnie's inclination was to take Sarah's statement at face value, partly because it was stated with such calm certitude, and partly because she was not sure whether there had been a change in Hobart, or if it was her own attitude toward him that had changed. It didn't occur to either of them that Sarah's attitude toward him might be what had changed.

The Visit

Ethel has aged tremendously—"overnight." Visiting her for the first time since her move to the nursing home, Helen doesn't recognize her at first. "What a shock!"

Frail, with snowy white hair, blue veins pulsing softly at her temples, a quavery voice ("Casey would waltz with the strawberry blonde," she sings, "while the band played on"), toothless, having mislaid her dentures ("That's what *they'll* tell you, dear, mislaid," she whispers slily, "but we know better, don't we? It's these nurses, oh, they take things. Watch out, hang onto your purse, dear, or you won't see it again—"), she is happy to see Helen. If it is actually Helen that she sees.

"Where is my dearest sister?" She clutches Helen's hand in her bony claw, pulls it to her cheek, kisses it. Helen's eyes are smarting, painful with unshed tears. She pats the hand, embraces the shrunken shoulder.

"She's as fragile as a bird—like the skeleton of a bird," Helen thinks with astonishment, still having in her mind's eye the picture of her stout, bustling, busy sister, whose voice, and even her peremptory little laugh, still issue from this shrivelled crone. Her knees tremble; she thinks her legs will give way, that she will burst into loud, shocking, uncontrollable sobs.

"I'll sit here and stay with you for a while," she says to Ethel. (Is it really Ethel?)

But Ethel is not unhappy. She laughs and sings, eats two pieces of the cake Helen has brought (at Tessie's suggestion), and with her skinny finger smooths and re-smooths the shiny, bright-colored wrappers of the sour candies she continually sucks.

"How beautiful it is," Helen hears her murmur to herself, eyes fixed on the shiny papers. "Beautiful, beautiful, beautiful."

A Special Providence

"There's no doubt about it," Tess says to Helen, the two of them reestablished in the apartment. "A special providence protects girls. Some of them do get raped and murdered, it's true, and it's horrible, but most of them don't. That's really the amazing thing! Because practically all of them act like Susie—look at yourself when you were her age."

Helen thinks, "What will happen to Susie?" And then she answers herself, "What happens to all of us, that's what. And that's what it's all about, isn't it? And she'll marry some ordinary young man—because Susie is an ordinary girl, isn't she? Like all of us, once upon a time."

Learning About the Earthquake

In the small room off the upstairs hall, Louise has noticed nothing. Not until after Hobart comes home, when they are sitting with their drinks in front of the television watching the news, does she learn about the earthquake.

"I can't believe I didn't feel anything," she says to Hobart, "but I was working, and you know how I am. Was anyone hurt?"

"They're still trying to assess the damage," Hobart tells her.

According to the National Earthquake Information Center, major destructive earthquakes are possible in sixteen states, including Missouri, Arkansas, Tennessee, California, Nevada, Washington, Montana, Wyoming, Utah, Mississippi, South Carolina, New York, Maine, Vermont, New Hampshire, and Massachusetts.

These possible sites were chosen on the basis of earthquakes felt in the United States dating back to 1663. Since that one, which occurred along what is now the St. Lawrence Seaway, there have been many major disturbances. The most profound probably occurred near New Madrid in southeast Missouri. The quakes reported there in 1811–1812 are regarded by experts as among the greatest in recorded history. Large areas of land sank, new lakes were formed, the Mississippi River channel altered its course, and 150,000 acres of forest were destroyed.

A Recognizable American

creeping out of the wreckage, bleeding, with broken limbs,
stumbling about in search of
"MOTHER" spelled out in pastel
bars of soap set in velvet, or
steel rods
tar
felt
gelatinous substances
(with two "bathing beauties")
and visions of demolished cars, victims of
suicide and bloody race riots
or dehumanizing portraits of
narcissistic movie stars
LOVE WAVE DISTORTION
supports these results
commensurate with agony
that stripped away from many steep

mountainsides all the mantle, with its cover
of forest, and blocked the adjacent valleys
with great heaps of waste

entirely mechanical, mass-produced !

After the earlier consolidation of the earth had been terminated by the Algoman folding, this major regeneration introduced the orthogenic synclines in which the orthotectonics of later times became

CONSUMER-ORIENTED

despite cries for help, screaming children, and the frantic
agonies of wounded animals, mules, horses, and
dogs
resulting from the fault-slip of the principal.
ALMOST NO ONE HAS EARTHQUAKE INSURANCE
. . . the ankh, the
Egyptian symbol for life, now
denoting sexual freedom.

Scientists at the University of Missouri at Rolla say it is possible that new seismic activity is occurring in the central United States, on a fault that parallels the New Madrid fault.

It seems like
a dream, or distant thunder
not supported by scientific evidence.